I0713602

BILLIONAIRE 43

Streaming Lovers, Book 2

Anna Lores

Blooming Cactus Publishing

To my soul sisters

ACKNOWLEDGEMENTS

———◆———

I HAVE SOME SPECIAL VIPS TO thank for a few names in this novella—Thank you, *Fran* for the surname Bell, *Marlene* for the surname Fox, and *Susan S.*, for the name Hudson. I appreciate your suggestions and am so happy with the outcome of the names in this story. Thank you to my fans. I adore you! I hope you love this installment of the Streaming Lovers series.

Thank you to my husband and kids for supporting me in my writing journey. This has been a year of ups and downs, but you've been my rock. Thank you to my friends, Denise, Kelly, and Tina. Y'all keep me focused on making my dreams come true.

Lastly, thank you, Kristi Cook, my fabulous editor for believing in this story. I appreciate your hard work and attention to detail. You polished this story until it shined. You are amazing!

CHAPTER ONE

———◆———

SOPHIA RICHLAND STARED AT THE kinky toy her best friend, Angie Winslow, fondled. *I'm not touching that.*

"This one feels real, don't you think?" Angie asked.

"Oh, yeah," Sophia said. "Look at those veins popping out and the size…A whole *three inches* like Kellen."

Angie burst out laughing. "He showed you his lack of goods again, huh?" she asked.

The humor Angie found in Kellen's need for constant validation of his manhood was lost on Sophia, but it was good to see her laugh. She'd been having a rough pregnancy. She and her husband Zane had been traveling all over the world with their kids to see if they could find something to help her gain weight instead of lose it.

"Yeah. It's getting on my nerves," Sophia replied.

Angie frowned. "It's part of your job."

"I know." Sophia released a half-sigh, half-groan. "I told him he'd never get hired at the club, but he keeps trying every penis enhancer under the sun—powder, gel, vitamin and toy—except surgery and nothing works for him. Thankfully, we don't take surgically enhanced dancers. And it's not a hookup club. The guys do not go home with patrons or other employees." Sophia repeated those same words a billion times over the five years she'd been working as the director of operations for the strip-club division of Jacob Bell Enterprises.

Angie rolled her eyes and put the dildo back on the shelf. She slid her hand over her undersized belly bump and sighed. "What size *are* you looking for?"

The warehouse she'd dragged Angie to on the search for the next hottest sex toy didn't seem to be working out. One last errand and Sophia was done. No more working for the boss she had been in love with for far too long. One more sex-toy decision and she never again had to worry about her choice losing the company money. "I don't know, but not Kellen sized. You're my expert."

The disappointment on Angie's face didn't help the situation.

"Angie, I measure and inspect dicks multiple times a day, three to five days a week. If anyone in the company knew I was a virgin, I'd have been out of a job in less than a heartbeat years ago. The last toy I picked out by myself didn't sell. We *lost* money. How was I supposed to know a fifteen-inch dick was too big?"

Another eye roll from Angie with the accompanying huff and slouch seemed a little much, even for her. "How many real fifteen-inch dicks have you ever touched?"

"None."

"There you go." Angie shook her head and seemed to struggle a little as they walked to the next aisle. "Get a size that matches or comes close to the measurements of the guys who bring the biggest crowds."

"That would have been nice information to have before now." Sophia picked up a toy with a clit stimulator. It was a little bigger than Kellen, but not—

"Not that one." Angie handed her a suction-cup cock and anal stimulator. "This one." She picked up an extra one from the shelf.

"You're buying one?" *Not with your hot husband ready at all times. He wouldn't go for that, would he?* "Do couples really use these?" *Do pregnant women use them?* She grabbed a few of the toys Angie picked out for the club.

"I am, and yes, couples do. Girl, you've got a lot to learn. I don't know how on earth you haven't been found out yet." Angie took Sophia's arm and leaned against her as they walked like little old ladies toward the warehouse saleswoman.

The brunette smiled as she held her tablet for orders. "I see you've decided on trying samples first?"

"We're trying samples," Angie said. "But Ms. Richland from Jacob Bell Enterprises is putting in a large order today."

"Thanks for referring your friend, Mrs. Winslow." The woman took each of the boxes Sophia held and scanned them. "This is a great choice for the club, Ms. Richland," the brunette said.

How do you know Angie? It was me who brought her, not the other way around. Sophia looked at the woman with the tablet. *Do you know I bought fifteen-inch dildos? Were you eavesdropping on us? Did you hear me talking about being a virgin?* She stood up as straight as she could to act confident and experienced in sex, even though she was neither at the moment. "I feel confident about today's choice in pleasure toy." Sophia negotiated the price as quickly as she could and left the warehouse with Angie.

As Sophia drove out of the parking lot and onto the barren desert road, nerves got the best of her. "I screwed up with that last order. I was able to return most of the products, but I'd made a huge judgement error. Jacob should have fired me." *I can't do this job anymore. I don't want to do it anymore. Why can't Jacob just fire me?*

"How much did you lose, really?"

"Does it matter? I lost the company money," Sophia said.

"Hundreds of thousands?"

"One thousand." Sophia's gut twisted. "I don't lose money on merchandise. Every time I think about it, I want to throw up."

"Girl, chill. You have nothing to worry about. I bet Jacob didn't bat an eye on that one. Not with the way you negotiate. You're scary when you get to talking numbers."

Jacob not only didn't bat an eye, he didn't even look at me when I handed him the report. The other toys still made up for the loss and some, but it was a loss and Jacob didn't forgive the smallest of bad investments. The hammer would fall at some point, and she didn't want to be the one hit.

"I'm handing Jacob my resignation letter today. I'm done. I can't lie to him anymore. I can't pull you away from your life to pick out sex toys for the club. I'm not qualified for this, and I'm never going to meet a man who wants a twenty-eight-year-old virgin and lots of babies."

"Quit the job, but tell Jacob you love him. Don't walk out of his office without clearly stating your feelings for him. I've told you this a thousand times, but I'm saying it again—I think he's crazy about you."

"If he were even slightly interested in me, he'd have done something about it by now. He takes what he wants, and he doesn't want me." She glanced at Angie. *You have the perfect life. Babies at home and one on the way. A billionaire husband who adores you. I'd settle for a job I don't hate and a baby growing inside me.*

"Are you taking your vacation days as part of your notice? Are you still opening the bakery with Hudson Fox?"

Sophia gazed at the city ahead and lightened her foot on the accelerator. "I'm doing both. I wasn't going to tell you because it's a secret, but I need to tell someone. I'm handing in my resignation tonight. I've added interviews for three qualified candidates to take my place on Jacob's calendar, and the bakery is ahead of schedule. It's ready to open now. Hudson says we can have a soft opening as soon as I'm ready, which is Monday."

"Oh, my goodness," Angie squealed. "I want a

sampling of cupcakes and cookies every day."

"There's more, Angie."

"There is?" She turned her whole body toward Sophia. "Spill. I want all the details. I can tell this is going to be juicy."

Sophia's cheeks burned, and she could feel the blood rising up to her forehead. She took a deep inhale and then exhaled. "I'm going on Pussy Pleasures as their Virgin Guest." *Call me Kitten to Billionaire 43.* "I'll be on tonight. I didn't want to explain to Jacob why I needed him to watch Rufus for me, so I checked Rufus in at a posh animal spa for the weekend. He's getting the royal treatment—doggy massages, baths, special treats, extra pettings, and even a television with all those cute puppy channels he loves to watch." She glanced at her friend.

Angie's mouth gaped wide. "You took Rufus to a spa?"

"Yes, and he loves it there. I took him for doggy play time a few times this month and he just hangs out and naps with whatever dog is tired out. It's really a special place. He is so happy there. And he's old, so they don't make him exercise or do anything he doesn't want to."

"Wait, wait, wait up." Angie touched Sophia's shoulder. "Did you say you're going on Pussy Pleasures?"

Here goes the hard part. You wouldn't understand this. You met Zane and he pounced all over you. No one has ever done that with me. "I want marriage and a husband someday, but for now, I'll settle for a baby to love and nurture—or, if I'm lucky, two or three children from the same man." *Watch out, Billionaire 43, I've signed every contract they gave me to ensure I have a family to love. Fingers crossed my fertility problems are solved with medication.*

The gentle touch of Angie's hand on Sophia's arm was comforting. "Are you sure about this?"

"I applied four months ago and got accepted after a bazillion tests. I seem to be a glutton for assholes when *I* try to find Mr. Right. This way, I won't have to deal with love or heartbreak. I'll have a man who wants to have a baby with me and will provide for our child or children. The bakery will provide me with a great opportunity to live my life on my own terms. Hudson is a great partner and, between the two of us, I know we can make it profitable. That's my biggest fear. I don't want to fail at what I love. On a good day, baking is wonderful. But on a bad day, it's my salvation."

"Your bakery is going to flourish. One taste of your peanut butter and chocolate protein cupcakes and…I need a cupcake."

Sophia laughed. "You're going to have to wait until Monday morning. Lis Greystoke has already placed a mammoth order and we're not even open yet. You might want to call yours in to my business answering machine, because I'm gonna be busy tonight and tomorrow."

"What if you don't get pregnant?" Angie asked.

"My breasts are killing me, they're so tender. I'm on hormones, and I'm about to ovulate. I have faith that I won't be the first Kitten who breaks Pussy Pleasures' one hundred percent success rate for pregnancy. Kitten and Billionaire 42 are having triplets. I believe everything I've done to this point will work."

I hope it works. Now, to face Jacob and fulfill the last requirement before heading home to prep for my Pussy Pleasures debut. Showing my breasts to Jacob will be easy. He won't even look at me. I'll flash him as he's reading my resignation letter. I'll tell him I love him under my breath as I'm walking out the door. Another moment of raw devastation avoided.

"Let Zane talk to Jacob. Don't you want your first time to be private and gentle?"

"This might sound strange to you, but I don't want gentle. I want someone to take me and take me hard. I asked for spanking and handcuffs and flogging. The only guy I considered losing my virginity to, besides Jacob, was a Dom who took me out to his club and spanked me. I came so hard in front of his junior Doms, my pussy squirted. I came even harder when all those tongues came out and took turns licking."

"Oh, my God," Angie mumbled. "Mr. I'm-going-to-make-you-come-so-hard-you'll-pass-out Trent?"

"Yeah," Sophia said. "Only, Trent and the Doms at his club don't do virgins, so my offer was quickly rejected…by all of them."

"*All of them*?" The shock in Angie's tone made Sophia feel a little better about herself.

"Yeah. Not the best experience of my life. I signed up for Pussy Pleasures when I got home. I'm done with dating. I'm done with my job. I'm done with my life as it is. I want to be a soccer mom. I want to cheer my kid on in whatever he or she does. I want to bring my child to work and teach him or her how to bake love into all the cakes and cookies and pastries we make."

She turned left into the parking deck of the corporate offices and parked in her space next to Jacob's. She inhaled and gazed at her best friend. "All I ever wanted to be was a mom with a minivan. The women at the office make fun of the life I would give my right arm to have. My life is dull. It doesn't sparkle. It doesn't shine. I want my life to—"

The familiar roar of Jacob's muscle car stopped Sophia from finishing. Her heart skipped a beat and her body decided now was the perfect time to turn on the burners. She clenched her jaw. *I do not want to want him anymore.*

The engine died and she waited to find out his mood by the way he shut his car door.

Slam. Open. Slam. Open. Slam.

Knock. Knock. Knock.

Sophia could barely breathe. *Your mood is making me glad I listened to my partner and bought the building for the bakery.* She swiveled in her seat and rolled down the window. *I should just tell you now that I quit.*

"Sophia, you're late," he stated. His hazel eyes looked like a storm brewed inside.

Her lips parted on a sharp inhale. "I'm not late." *What? You didn't get sex last night?*

"It's four-thirty. You're late. You're an hour late. An. Hour. I went out looking for you. Where have you been?" He glanced in the car and his voice and glare softened. "Hi, Angie. How're you feeling? Zane said you went to a new doctor this morning?"

Sophia turned her head and gazed at Angie. *I thought you were doing better. Why didn't you tell me you went to see a doctor?* "Is the baby okay?"

"Doing fine," Angie said. She looked at Jacob. "Yeah. Took some bloodwork and scheduled some more tests. Sophia made me lunch, and I do really well whenever she cooks, so…" Angie opened her door and slipped out of the car. She bent over and grabbed the sex toy box from the floorboard. "I'll talk to you later." She closed the door and seemed to find the energy to hustle to her car two rows back.

"Turn off your car and come with me. Now." The angry Jacob she preferred to avoid reared his head and opened her car door. "Hurry, Sophia. I need to talk to you in my office."

"Fine." She shut off her car, stuffed the boxes in her extra-large tote, picked up her small purse, and exited her car. She handed the bag to Jacob. "You're being mean, so you have to hold my purse, too."

He carried her bags and slammed her car door.

"Be careful, Jacob," she said. "That is my property."

He growled.

She shuddered and nearly stumbled as she stepped forward, leading the way. *I hate that you turn me on when you're like this. That sound. God, stop making that sound.*

His arm snaked around her waist. The warmth from his body, of being so close, weakened her knees.

"You're late. You set the appointment for the end of day. Everyone is gone. You didn't answer your phone. You scared the shit out of me." He typed in the code to enter and opened the door to his building. "Walk straight to my office. Do not pass go. Do not stop at the ladies' powder room. Do not make one small detour. Understand?"

"Yes, sir." *You're going to make quitting easy on me. Real. Easy.*

She strode down the hallway, wove through the cubicle maze, the lobby, and into the executive suites to Jacob's corner office.

The door closed and the beautiful pinks, oranges, and reds of the desert sunset illuminated the masculine room.

"I've heard rumors," Jacob said. "Did Kellen drop his drawers and demand you measure him again this morning?"

"Yes," she said.

"I figured that fifteen-inch dildo you picked out for your latest favorite sex toy would have been enough of a hint you're not into him," Jacob said. "Damn it. He's certifiably crazy."

Jacob strode behind his desk and placed her bags on the smooth, granite top. "You should have come to me. I don't want you dealing with that shit. You are a beautiful woman and a target for creeps like that."

He picked up the receiver to his office phone and hit the numbers with his finger as if he were punching someone. "Did they catch Kellen? If he comes within five miles of Sophia I will tear off his dick and feed it to him. You should have protected her from him. I pay you to protect her and that fucker was banned from my clubs six months ago. Why the hell was he allowed in? Why was he within 500 feet of the entrance to the test club?"

Sophia stared at the man who wasn't a stranger to strong emotions, but whatever had him worked up today, he was on a war path, and she seemed to be the one he was fighting to protect.

"Jacob, it's okay," she said. "He's not that kind of threat. He's wants to be a—"

His pale skin flushed fire-engine red. "He did what!?!"

She zipped her lips and stood up straight. *Oh shit. What happened? Did Kellen spill a little on the new guy checking cocks?*

His hand shook and the veins in his neck visibly throbbed. "When I come back, this place better be cleaned out of all the fuckers who knew or suspected...or so help me God, I will close all my clubs down and ruin every damn person who ever had contact with him and his associates." He slammed the phone down. He hung his head, his eyes closed. His hands dropped flat to the modern, gray granite desktop, and rage seemed to consume him. He breathed heavily through several cycles before his hands stopped shaking.

She waited.

And waited.

And.

Waited.

"I'm going to...uh, go home," she whispered.

He raised his head and opened his eyes. The gray hues lightened inside the dominant green and light brown of his irises, but the turmoil that always accompanied the subtle change in color remained. "You can't go home. Your apartment was broken into. Do you know where your dog is?"

Her heart stopped. "Rufus is at the doggy spa."

"Please check if he's still there."

"He is. I dropped him off this morning and checked on him twice." She grabbed her purse and turned it over. "He's staying there while I'm gone."

She shook her purse and the contents scattered across the cold granite in what seemed like deafening clanks — lip gloss, notebooks, pens, work and personal tablets, keys, and Rufus's collar. She gave it one more shake and her phone hit the unyielding stone and bounced into her hand.

A large crack from the initial blow expanded in all directions and spread across the screen. Her reflection in the shattered black glass scared her. Rufus was her life, her love, her baby. She'd had him for twelve years.

She tapped and tapped against the black glass until her image disappeared and Rufus's sweet brown and black terrier mix face appeared. *They would never let anyone take Rufus. Not without calling me. Not without calling Hudson. Rufus is safe. He's safe. He has to be.*

Somehow the phone continued to work, but each firm touch sent more cracks through the webbed mess, sure to break it. Frantically, she scrolled through her texts. *Nothing. Nothing. Nothing.*

Her heart stopped.

In a split second, the air exited the space she occupied.

One. Buried. Text.

No.

No. No. No.

Cancellation. Release.

She read the words again as the room tipped on its side. *Cancellation. Release.*

"They released him. Someone stole my dog." She dialed the number as her world fell apart.

"This is—"

Jacob tapped the screen of his phone. "Shit," he mumbled.

"Is Rufus Richland still there? It's Sophia. I dropped him off this morning. I called two hours ago to make sure he had his baby reindeer toy. Please tell me there wasn't a mistake and you didn't release my dog to a stranger."

"He's with your boyfriend."

"I don't have—"

"Oh, stop," the woman on the other end said. "Your secret is out. Congratulations on your engagement. Kellen is handsome and sweet, and that note you wrote to release Big Ruff to him…"

I don't call him Big Ruff. No one calls my Rufus anything but the name I gave him twelve years ago when I found him. Sophia couldn't breathe. She stared at the phone. *This is not happening.*

Jacob hurdled his desk and wrapped her up in his arms. He slid the phone from her hand. "This is Jacob Bell. Please call the police."

Her heart and soul broke as Jacob voiced the truth she feared hearing. *Kellen…Kellen, the nice guy with a small dick took my dog and broke into my home and murdered him.* Sobs wrecked her professional veneer.

"Baby, I'm so sorry. I'm so sorry," Jacob whispered. "I'm so sorry."

She curled into his embrace and continued to cry.

"We'll get him. He'll go to jail for what he's done. My attorneys will make sure of it."

I should have brought Rufus with me. While I was shopping for sex toys I don't know anything about, he was taken by a lunatic. "I need to talk to the police. There has to be a mistake. He couldn't have hurt my fur baby."

"It's not a mistake. Rufus is gone. He's gone. I'm so sorry."

She shook her head. "No. He's not…Kellen couldn't have. Wouldn't have. He's not…" *Oh, God. My Rufus was dying while I… No. I won't believe it. I can't.*

"It's true, baby. I'll take care of everything. I'll make sure his body is—"

"No. I'm going to believe in miracles. I'm going to believe in them, no matter how messed up Kellen might be." *Only the sickest of people do that. Kellen was nice. Kellen was NICE.* "How do you know Kellen broke into my home? He may have wanted a date with me, but he wouldn't hurt my dog because I wasn't interested. Rufus would've torn him apart."

Jacob's phone vibrated and rang out in his chief of security's ringtone.

Sophia backed away as Jacob answered. *I'm done. I'm so done. Rufus. No. Not my sweet protector. Not my constant companion. Is this the universe telling me I am a terrible person? Why would he be taken away from me?*

"Tell me what you know," he said. He pulled her into his arms once again. "The police have

Kellen in custody. He stopped at a doctor's office to be stitched up from dog bites. They sent him to the hospital. Photos of you were everywhere in Kellen's home. Everywhere. Listen to me, Sophia. Listen, and stop thinking for a minute."

"I quit, Jacob. I'm done here. I—"

"You're not quitting. I'll give you any job you want in my organization, but you're not quitting over this. You are working for me."

"I'm leaving for good…I won't be back Monday. I'm done. I'm beyond done." She cinched her bottom lip with her teeth and looked up at him. "I don't want to live like this anymore. I lost my dog because I can't read people's intentions. I don't know shit about sex or toys or anything. I'm a virgin, for goodness sake."

His mouth softened and the cock pressed against her belly hardened and grew. "You shouldn't resign, not now."

"So, you're accepting my resignation?" Her chin crinkled and her lips trembled. She backed away from him. *I can't put my heart or anything else on the line ever again. I'm done with you, with this job. I lost my dog because of this place.*

"Not now, I'm not. Reschedule your vacation. You need to grieve."

I promised Rufus I would bring home a baby he could love and protect, and now…

Another round of sobs took over, and she found herself cuddled in the safety and comfort of Jacob's arms once again.

"Shh, I've got you. I'm going to get your apartment boxed up and cleaned. You're not seeing what that man did. I'll handle everything.

I'll keep you safe. You can count on me."

"I can't," she whispered. *I can't count on anyone but myself.* "I have to get out of here. Out of this place."

"Sophia, no vacation is so urgent you have to—"

"This is. There are no refunds. No second chances. If I don't show up tonight, my one chance at having a baby is gone. Gone. You don't get it because you can and do whatever you please. You have the funds, the connections, the…*everything.*" She pushed away from him. "I'm not working for you anymore."

His eyes dropped to her chest and lust settled into his gaze. "Okay. If that is your decision, I accept your resignation."

"Eyes up here." She pointed at her face. "God, what is wrong with you? My dog is…I don't even know how to—"

"I know." He made a growling noise. "When you're around, you make me so fucking insane, Sophia. No matter what else is going on, good, bad or fucking horrible…" His tongue caressed along his bottom lip as he continued staring at her chest.

She looked down and her blouse had unbuttoned, her breasts bared to him. "Take a good look because it is never happening again. Ever." *I can't do a once and done thing with you. It would kill me. I'm never going to be your friend with benefits.*

"I think I'll be seeing them a lot now that you don't work for me. You'll be needing someone to fuck while you're pregnant, and I'm the perfect guy for you."

You don't know how true that is. "Let me tell

you something, Jacob. You're talking about sex while my world has been turned upside down." *And I'm thinking about that bulge in your pants and wishing it was you who was making love to me for the first time. Wishing I had asked you to take care of Rufus. Wishing it was you I could come home to, not stay with for a night. I don't want a night with you. I want forever. I'm not even going to give you the satisfaction of telling you I love you.* "And you think I'll come crawling to you for sex?"

"More like waddling," he said. "You'll definitely be one of those sexy moms. I see a minivan overflowing with children. Ruf-Mistress Bark will have to keep all those wild children in line."

She crossed her arms over her chest. *You're being sweet. Trying to make me feel better. I might borrow Mistress Bark from you when I get back.* She cracked a smile. *She loved my boy Rufus. He loved her.*

The truth of Kellen's crimes, of Rufus's death, hit her then. If Jacob believed Rufus had passed on, then her fur baby had. Jacob loved dogs as much as she did. He wouldn't lie or even suggest it if he wasn't one hundred percent sure. The truth drove a nail into her heart and into Rufus's coffin.

He gripped her hips. "Let me suck those titties, Sophia. I'll get you so hot, you won't have any pain when my big cock pops your sweet cherry. You won't need to go to a sperm clinic." He thrust his hips. "I got all the sperm you need right here."

"Sorry, Jacob. These *titties* are for my future husband." She dragged her arms across her breasts and rubbed her nipples with the palm of her hands. "These *big titties* are only for his hands, his mouth, his cock." She twisted and pinched the tight buds. "I like a rough touch and I'm not sure you're up to my standards."

He growled. "Those titties are mine to play with however I please. Soft and sweet or rough and dirty." He leaned over and kissed her neck. "You're a virgin I want to fuck. I want to take your raven hair and wrap it around my hand. You'll do whatever I want, whenever I want, wherever I want."

This isn't real. "You're only doing this because I—"

"Sophia," he whispered. "I'm going to take you to my house, and we're going to burn up the sheets tonight."

Her heart pounded so fast and hard, she wasn't sure if she was in the throes of a heart attack or about to have the orgasm to end all orgasms. Either way, he never said he loved her. If he had said he loved her, she'd go home with him, make a baby, do whatever, whenever, wherever with him, but he hadn't. She'd rather have sex with a bachelor, billionaire stranger who wanted her to carry his baby than have sex with Jacob who would toss her out of his house and home as soon as she managed to live without her big dog Rufus in her life.

He pulled her flush against him. "I'm going to make you forget about this awful day and give you something to look forward to." He squatted and hoisted her up in his arms, and shifted her around. He pushed the contents of her purse off the top of his desk.

She landed softly on her back on the hard granite.

"I've wanted this for a long time," he mumbled. "I never thought you were a virgin. You're so… so…" His eyelids fell, covering most of his gorgeous eyes.

She turned her head and saw the time. *One hour. I need to leave now. I'm going to change my circumstances. I'll mourn Rufus and deal with reality when I get back.*

"No. We're not doing this." She covered her chest. "I've got to go." She scissored her legs up, to the side, and down to the floor.

"We are going to do this," he said. "Where are you going?"

She bolted to the door and pulled it open. "I'm going to the one opportunity in my life that will bring me happiness." *I'm going to star on Pussy Pleasures and make a baby.*

Without looking back, she held her breasts and ran until she got in her car. She drove to her apartment like she was in the race of her life, all the while praying Jacob lied and Kellen, for whatever reason, brought her dog home and left him there, safe and sound.

CHAPTER TWO

Jacob

I SHOULDN'T HAVE TAKEN HER INTO my office. I should have made her get in my car and taken her to my house. I should have told her I loved her. That I can't live without her. That I'd protect her and make sure nothing bad ever happened to her again. Then I wouldn't be here naked wearing a mask and blue colored contacts.

Knock. Knock.

"I'm almost ready," Jacob said. "But you can come in." He picked up his shoes and placed them on the bottom of the wardrobe cabinet. He slipped off his college ring and placed it on the shelf above his suit.

The doctor he'd gotten to know over the last few weeks stepped into the dressing room. He shoved his hands in the large pockets of his open, white lab coat. Blue scrubs and running shoes finished off the good doctor's outfit. The man was the best fertility specialist in the country, bar none. Zane Winslow had to have paid him an inordinate amount of money to join Pussy Pleasures, which meant the live-stream made plenty to cover the financial margins.

"Thanks for telling us what happened to her dog and her home," Dr. Bledwell said. "We can reschedule Kitten 43's pregnancy announcement to accommodate any changes in her schedule due to the circumstances."

"How is she?" Jacob asked.

"She's upset, but she's one of our most mentally strong kittens. She's pushing it aside, for now. But when the shock is over and reality hits her, it will probably knock her down for a little while." Dr. Bledwell nodded as if he were talking to himself.

He looked up at Jacob and fished a stethoscope from one of the pockets. He put it over his shoulders at the base of his neck and held each end with one hand. "Now, let's talk about you. Are you ready for this? She might cry, even though she knows what is going to happen. I think she might want to be punished, so tread that path lightly, if you choose to take that path at all."

"I'm ready." *She needs to cry. I hope Zane is right, and she does love me like I love her. I'm a damn idiot for not telling her. If she doesn't love me, I'm fucked seven days 'til Sunday.*

"Good. You have to hurry. She's ovulating."

"But I thought we needed to get her before she started so my guys had some time to wait around for one of her eggs to mature." His heartbeat increased. *What if she doesn't get pregnant? Will she want me then? I'm not losing her because of some timing issue.* "Maybe we should reschedule until next month. This couldn't be happening at a worse time."

"She doesn't want to wait. If you're not up for this, we have someone who is. He's here, and he's in love with her, too."

"Who?" *He's not touching my woman.*

"That's confidential. I need your decision now."

"Show me the way, Doc. I'm ready to claim my prize." Jacob fisted his cock. *I've got to marry her before anyone else gets the chance. She has no idea how special and unique she is.*

Doctor Bledwell turned around. "Follow me."

Jacob trekked behind the man in the white coat out of the room and down a wide hall with mounted cameras on tracks.

"Once you show proof she was a virgin, get back in her and fill her up with your sperm. You have a short window of time before the opportunity to fertilize one or more of her eggs this month is gone."

"No pressure, right?" *Shit.*

"I've heard you perform best when the odds are stacked against you."

"Is that what people say?" *Does Zane say that about me?*

The doc stepped to the side. "Yes, they do. They also say that you close deals no one else can."

And they are right. "Huh."

A man in cargo shorts and an army green tee walked forward. "I'm Evan, the director." He grabbed the bill of his black baseball cap and squeezed the edges together. "We have a team at Sophia's cleaning up and making an inventory of the items that need to be replaced. We don't know what to do about her dog's beds, toys, food, and doggy dresser."

"Wash and box it up. Everything is going to be delivered to my house."

"Okay. Also, since this is a special circumstance, we've announced to our subscribers that a tragedy struck our latest Kitten and the streak of pregnancies might come to an end. We did mention her dog being stolen and dying, but not the circumstances. There are requests for you to find her a puppy immediately."

"She likes older dogs," Jacob said. "And she picks them out herself."

"Special circumstances," Evan said. "Either you find her the perfect puppy, or Pussy Pleasures will do it."

I'll have to get Angie on that one. She's puppy rescue central. "Anything else?"

"Yeah. Careful with her nipples. The piercer just left the set."

Jacob's cock jerked and cum trickled from the tip. "I didn't think she'd do that."

"She did, and she's waiting." Evan nodded to the right and began walking with him. "You ready?"

"Don't I look ready?"

Evan chuckled. "Yeah, man. Remember to call her 'Kitten'. And do a quick show of your dick before you get back in her pussy and shoot your load. There can't be any doubt she's a virgin."

Whatever. Jacob ignored him and lengthened his stride. *I'm done waiting.*

"And, Jacob," Evan said. "The medication this month didn't work very well on her. It's an uphill hike across rugged terrain to the top of Mount Everest, and you're starting in a locked submarine at the bottom of the ocean."

Sonofabitch. Probably one egg available and an hour to get it fertilized. No tit action. Now I've got to get a puppy she will love, keep the heat on my security team to dig up everything they can find on Kellen Pruitt, and give it all to the police for a solid and quick conviction. Anything else to add to my never-ending impossible list of things to do?

He nodded at the cameramen and followed their hand gestures to—

"*Fuck*," he mumbled.

Lubed with her own juices, Sophia posed with her long, lean legs wide and her pussy on display. Her big tits shined with sparkling diamonds around her nipples. Her palms pressed against the white area rug at the foot of the bed.

The rest of the room faded around him. *Mine.* He crossed the room.

"Safe, sane, and consensual," Evan said over the pounding of Jacob's heart.

"Fuck my pussy. Turn the crimson blood white with your cleansing cum," Sophia whispered the words all the kittens before her had spoken before their first time with their lover. Her legs trembled.

I know you're scared, baby. I'm going to take care of you. He wanted to go easy, work her up and make her orgasm before he even tried to get his cock inside her, but the show demanded immediate proof and a caveman-style taking.

He gripped her hips and, without a word, thrust as hard as he could manage.

She screamed and her muscles contracted, but it was too late. He was in and buried deep.

He would have waited, let her adjust to having a cock inside her for the first time, but he didn't have time. He had a job. Pregnancy was the goal, and he had the ball and was going to run it into the end zone come Hell or high water. No one could out-work him.

She gasped as he pulled out.

"Yeah," Evan said. "Our pretty Virgin Kitten isn't a virgin anymore."

Shut the fuck up, Evan. She's mine. Not yours or Pussy Pleasures' Kitten. She's mine. Only. Mine.

Jacob grunted as he thrust into her center. He had to take her and get her orgasming fast and often. Get her body to demand his cum and pull his sperm into the flow of fluids straight to that egg. *You want a baby? I'm gonna give you one.*

Her belly tightened and her pussy walls embraced him. "You're big. Huge."

Not fifteen-inches huge. He grinned. *But yeah, Sophia, a solid nine inches for your pleasure.* He pulled her left leg over his thigh.

She twisted her hips and adjusted her hands. "What are you…?"

He slid his hand along her leg to her hip and over her belly to her mons. He glided his middle finger between her wet folds to the swollen bud and rubbed back and forth. Back and forth. Back and forth.

"Mmm," she moaned.

He supported her hip with his right hand and thrust in fast, short pumps as he roughly worked to sensitize her clit, back and forth, side to side, around and around.

Her moans amped up his libido.

"Yes," she panted. "Oh, God. Oh. God. Yes."

He tapped her clit and thrust. Those sweet walls

gripped his cock like a vise. Her legs seemed to weaken, and he accepted more and more of her weight.

That's it, baby, surrender to me. Surrender to me, and I'll let you know it's me. I'm here to make every one of your dreams come true.

She gasped. "I'm sorry. I'm sorry. I'm going to…"

He pushed the pad of his finger into the center of her clit and dragged it down. Her pussy clamped like a bear trap around his girth. His balls tightened. *I'm going to come.*

"Yes," she shouted. A shudder ran through her and her arms wobbled, but he lifted her as he thrust and let go of his seed.

He thrust and thrust and thrust, holding her, twisting her hips, and giving her the sperm she so desperately wanted inside her.

Sweet juices coated his balls and his hand. His beautiful Sophia trusted him to support and protect her while they made love. His cock slid semi-hard from her and ready to get hard and try again.

As he maneuvered her limp and satisfied body into his arms and onto the bed, he noticed a goofy smile on her face. He carefully raised each of her arms over her head and slipped her wrists into the fur-lined handcuffs attached to the top corner posts of the bed.

She kept her eyes closed and a sexy smile on her face as he spread her legs and wrapped thicker cuffs around her ankles. "Mmm. More."

He lowered over her until his chest pressed against hers and his cock lined up nicely at her sex. He kissed her forehead. "I like the diamonds on your titties," he whispered. "Too bad you just got that done. I wanted to suck them until you came."

Her lids shot open and the fake green contacts didn't hide the surprise and recognition inside them. She tugged at her arms and legs, but he had her secured well.

"You. You're here? You're here. You're really here."

He dipped closer and whispered into her ear, "In the flesh. I have to say I'm disappointed you didn't recognize me earlier." *Tell the truth, Sophia. You did recognize me, but you didn't trust your gut.*

"I'll tell you a secret," she said.

You're speaking loud enough for the audience to hear. Why? "I love confessions," he said.

"I fantasized it was you," she said.

"It's break time," Evan interrupted. "Live stream will recommence in forty minutes." He shoved pillows under her hips. "Twenty minutes like this. It's protocol." He walked off set.

Jacob kissed her ear. "You're my first and last virgin."

"You're an asshole," she said. "Sorry it was so bad I turned you off from making love to vir—"

"You didn't turn me off. I'm going to make you mine," he interrupted. "I'm going to be the only man you're ever taking into your body's orifices. The only man you'll ever know intimately."

"And how is that fair? You've fucked a thousand girls or more," she huffed.

"I'm not a man whore," he said. "Not everyone I dated got my cock. None of them got me bare.

None of them were worthy of the title of fiancée, wife, or mother of my children."

"Well, I'm not any of those things and the last one is probably not happening. So, don't get your hopes up. The only label you'll have in my life is being *my first*."

You think I'm going to leave you? Abandon you? I'm not leaving. You're getting all those titles in the weeks to come. He lifted into a half pushup and gazed into her eyes. "Will you marry me?"

"Stop teasing. It's not funny."

"I'm serious," he said. "Will you marry me?"

She rolled her eyes. "*Sure…*" She seemed to leave off the "asshole" at the end of her acceptance to his proposal, but he didn't care.

I'm not walking out of here until you're my wife. "Evan, get the marriage license filed and someone to marry us ASAP," he shouted.

She gasped and jerked at the chains. "I didn't sign a marriage license. I didn't do—" Her cheeks flushed pink. Dawning of all the paperwork she had signed was written all over her face. "The paperwork. I signed all the paperwork."

"Yes, you did." He grinned. "I did too. Let's do this. Me and you." He lunged forward and thrust his throbbing cock into her sticky, wet center. *I've got to fuck you as often as possible to give you a baby.*

She bit her bottom lip and moaned. "Yes," she mumbled.

He wasn't sure if she had really agreed to marry him, or if the feel of his cock pumping inside her made her voice her pleasure. "You're going to be my wife." He rocked back and powered into her.

She squeezed her thighs, but the restraints kept her legs perfectly splayed for his musings.

With her pussy open and available for him to do anything he wanted, his cock hardened more than it ever had in his life. *Mine. You're finally going to be my wife. My wife.*

He reached up and interlocked his fingers with hers. "As soon as you say 'I do' I'm going to pump so much cum into your pussy, in nine months you'll be giving birth to twins."

"Oh, my God. I do. I do. I fucking *do.*"

Her walls gripped his cock with a strength that weakened his knees and at the same time strengthened him with a primal need to procreate. He rose above her and slammed into her as her walls relaxed between the delicious contractions. "You want my cum?"

"Yes, sir," she moaned.

"Here it comes, baby." He sucked in a breath as his balls clenched and tingled. A jolt of energy shot like a laser from his groin and up his shaft. He grunted with the last thrust and let loose a low grumble. He squeezed his glutes and released his sperm to swim along her rapids to her womb. For the first time since *his* first time, he relished the experience. His dick jerked and spurted into the woman he had wanted for far too long.

Her pussy seemed hotter, tighter, and hungrier this time. Maybe it was the confirmation he was Billionaire 43, or maybe it was his skill. Whatever the reason, the beauty of her orgasms, the consent and submission of her will, the trust she gave him made him want to have her pregnant with his child now more than ever.

"Repeat after me," came a man's voice, pulling him from the pleasure of claiming his woman. "I, Kitten 43, vow to love, honor, be faithful, loyal and obedient to my Pussy Pleasures' Billionaire 43 for the rest of my days on earth for as long as we both shall live."

Sophia's voice sounded sexy as sin as she repeated the words.

Jacob's cock demanded attention to finish the job he refused to continue, but he wouldn't give in to its desires until he had what he needed – Sophia as his wife.

"Billionaire 43?" the man said.

Jacob glanced toward the sound of the voice and saw a man in a business suit and tie wearing a masquerade mask similar to his and Sophia's. "Yes?"

The tall, slender man strode forward and handed him a wedding band. "For your kitten."

With his cock buried inside Sophia, he took the ring and slipped it onto her finger.

"Repeat after me," the man said. "I, Pussy Pleasures' Billionaire 43, vow to love, honor, be faithful and loyal to Pussy Pleasures' Kitten 43 for the rest of my days on earth for as long as we both shall live."

Jacob repeated the vow.

"Care to untie one of her restraints so she can place a ring on your finger to show the world you are hers?" the man asked.

Jacob slipped the cuff from the chain attached to a D-ring on the headboard of the bed.

The man handed the wedding band to Sophia. Her hand trembled, but she slid the symbol of their lifetime commitment onto his ring finger.

The officiant spoke of their bond together as husband and wife, then Evan broke away from the live-stream.

The man said, "I now pronounce you husband and wife. Congratulations, Mr. and Mrs. Jacob Bell."

"Thanks," Jacob answered. He gave Sophia a peck on the lips. "How do you feel, Mrs. Bell?"

"That was real?" she whispered.

Jacob nodded.

"Yes, Mrs. Bell," the officiant said. "You're now a married woman. I'll leave you two to continue where you left off." He walked off the set and out of view.

"I'm really married to you?" she asked. "But, I didn't sign a prenup. And neither did you."

"Are you planning on divorcing me?" he asked.

Her jaw dropped. "I. Uh, no."

He unhooked her other wrist from the chain. "Stay where you are." His cock slid from her warmth as he shifted and sat up. He slipped the restraints from around her ankles and climbed from the bed.

"Where are you going?" she asked.

"It's a surprise." He sauntered across the bedroom set to Evan. He needed to check out the shower area to see if it would accommodate the fantasy he had planned to make real. Plus, his dick needed to remember who was boss.

She might be fertility challenged, but he overcompensated in that department. If there was an egg available, he wasn't letting it go to waste. Not when he finally had the woman of his dreams claimed and ready to start a family. Not when he needed to give her something to look forward to as she grieved for Rufus over the weeks and months to come.

"Everything okay?" Evan asked.

"I'd like to prepare and inspect the bathroom."

"It's ready," Evan said.

"I'll decide if it's ready." Jacob glanced at the cameramen and then at Evan. "Who is going to point me in the right direction?"

"Second door on the left," Evan said. "Newly renovated with a four-person tub and shower."

"Thank you." *Perfect.* "Are my bath toys washed and at their stations?"

Evan nodded. "Cleaned and packaged the way you requested."

"Good." Jacob strode onto the set. "Kitten, your surprise is almost ready." He didn't wait for her answer—instead, he opened the door to the bathroom and entered. His cock hardened. *Zane, you're one thorough fucker.*

CHAPTER THREE

Sophia

SOPHIA SLID HER LEGS THROUGH the soft, gel-filled tethers at the end of the bench and carefully maneuvered to her knees. Lowering her torso flush against the specially designed bench in the four-person shower sent a thrill through her and lessened the burden of fear that she wasn't or possibly might never be pregnant. *I want a baby. I want a little boy with your hazel eyes and my dark hair. I want him to stand on a stool wearing an apron in my bakery and get flour all over the kitchen as he mixes cupcake batter.*

Jacob tightened the straps spreading her thighs apart. His fingers glided up and teased the edges of her sensitive pussy lips. "You're a very obedient wife."

Are you really my husband or was all that a joke? We didn't use real names, not until the end, and then only yours. Who was that guy? Nothing seemed official. Was that all a stunt for ratings? There is no way they could get someone here that quickly. She gripped the handles built into the white powder-coated metal legs of the bench. *This is insane. All of it.*

Her heart pummeled against her ribcage as she fidgeted to get comfortable. This way and that, she squirmed as she lay chest-down against the blue padded bench in the shower. The swollen tips of her nipples rubbed against the smooth, waterproof surface. The movement drew more blood to the surface from the friction of her nipple jewelry. She wasn't sure she could handle whatever he had planned for her. *You're insatiable. Will you always be like this? Want me like this?*

"Kitten, I've given you milk here." Jacob dipped two digits deep into her pussy. "You haven't swallowed it all."

She squeezed her pussy walls around his fingers. "I'm sorry, sir. I'll do better next time." She drew in her bottom lip and held it to stop from moaning. *I want to experience your rougher side. I watched you with other women. You weren't gentle. You took what you wanted, and they loved it.*

"Will you do better?" He curled his fingers and extended them, rubbing back and forth.

She shuddered as an orgasm rose up and hovered just out of reach. *You've been playing me all this time. You have been exploring my body and reactions. You've been learning and using that knowledge to—*

"Answer me," he demanded.

She wouldn't be able to hold onto the handles when she orgasmed. She *would* fall into bliss and let go. *You know I don't know what I'm doing.* "Yes, sir."

"Mmm." He pulled his fingers from her center

and lightly swatted her right bottom cheek.

She squeaked and let go of the handles as her body jerked from the unexpected contact.

He squatted beside her. "Be a good kitten and hold on."

She closed her fingers around the handles but stayed vigilant to his position near her. Everything about him kept her on edge, waiting for his next move.

"Good kitty." He inhaled. "That didn't hurt, did it?"

"No, sir. Surprised me, that's all." *How rough will you get with me? Will you make me cry?*

"I'll spank your sexy ass when it's offered so freely. Have you changed your mind about being gently introduced to rougher forms of play?"

The warmth of his hand on her back soothed some of the tension she held. "I haven't changed my mind. I want to experience all you have to offer. All of it." *I might pass out from orgasmic bliss or ugly crying, but I want to understand the kind of sex you want and need.*

The ripping of a material that sounded like plastic made her back stiffen and her entire body flex. She turned her head but couldn't see what he was doing. *Please don't let it be fifteen inches long. Please, don't do that to me.*

The spring of a pump heightened her senses. *What are you doing?*

"My kitten says she wants to experience all I have to offer, but that is going to take years."

Smack.

She jerked harder against the special straps than the spank warranted. *I'm too jumpy. Too on edge.*

No matter what he does, I'm not giving him the satisfaction of—

His fingers separated her bottom cheeks.

Shit. No. Not that. I don't remember signing off on anal play. "I don't think so."

"What? You said you wanted to experience all I have to offer. Are you afraid, kitten?"

You're a fuckwad. I can't believe you're actually doing this to me live. "No, lover. I'm not afraid of anything."

"Nothing?"

Smack.

"Tell the truth," he growled.

Damn, that noise turned her on and her body responded like a lioness in heat. She wasn't about to tell the truth. She wouldn't tell him sleeping anywhere without her dog scared her. She wasn't about to let him know that she took Rufus to the cock-measuring sessions during the week. That Rufus accompanied her almost everywhere. Everywhere but the sex toy stores. He had stayed in the car with the windows rolled down. Or, he had jumped out of the truck and waited patiently by the entrance for her to come out. *I'll never have as perfect a companion as you, Rufus.*

Tears clouded her eyes and her judgement. *If I hadn't worked for Jacob's night club line, I never would have met Kellen. I wouldn't have lost the best dog in the entire world. The best dog I've ever had. My one-in-a-billion dog best friend. My Rufus would still be alive.*

She closed her eyes and held back the sobs ready to break free. *I'm not falling to pieces in public. I'm not. I won't.*

"I'm not afraid of anything, sir." Somehow she managed to keep the emotions roiling inside the cauldron of her heart from leaking out in her voice.

"Huh."

She hated that non-questioning word he used when he noticed something or was conversing internally.

"If you're not going to be honest, we're not playing this game today."

Damn it. I need this game. I want this game. I want to be spanked so hard I can cry from the strike of his hand, not the misery of losing my fur baby. I want to feel something other than despair. I want to forget about reality. Push away the pain of losing my fearless and perfect companion. I want to be punished for my choices. "I'm afraid of going home to an empty house. I'm afraid of finding out the details of what happened to my dog. My wonderful protector. My constant companion." Tears slipped out from between her lids. "Please do something. Anything. Don't leave me like this."

Jacob's hand landed softly against her bottom and glided up her back to her neck. He kissed her shoulder. "I will never leave you. I'm going to be your protector, your companion, your lover, your husband, the father of your children. You're not going home to an empty house. You're coming home with me."

She bit the inside of her cheek to stop from dipping beneath the waves of grief. *I'm making a baby. It's not time to think about anything but getting through this moment.*

Pushing the thoughts of her dog to the back of

her mind, she released the inside of her cheek and exhaled. "No more games, sir. Do whatever you have planned. I'll surrender to you."

"You didn't agree to anal play," Jacob whispered. "But you'd let me do it, wouldn't you?"

"No, sir. I wouldn't," she whispered. But she would. No matter what he wanted that scared her, she trusted the goodness inside him that he wouldn't intentionally harm her. He was a good man.

"I'll have to change your mind, kitten."

"Not in this lifetime." *Get angry with me. Lose your temper.*

"Huh."

There was that sound. He was too perceptive. *Just punish me so I feel better. I deserve worse than a little spank and flog. I—*

He kissed her neck. "I'm asking for a break. You're not yourself. I'm worried about you."

"No," she whispered. "Please. I don't want a break. I want this to be over. I want to make a baby and go. Spank me or something. I will do anything you want. I just need you to finish this. Please?"

The heat of his body disappeared. No hot breath against her flesh. No whispers. No gentle kisses.

He spread her nether lips.

She squeaked as something pinched her clit. *Shit. Not clamps. I didn't want clamps. He put a clamp on me. He actually put a damn clamp on my clit.*

Thwack.

She gasped as her bottom burned.

Thwack.

She held her breath for another. *Don't hit the clamp. Don't hit the clamp.*

Thwack. Thwack. Thwack.

Five more in a sequence of slow, slow, fast, fast, fast.

The tip of his cock touched her pussy and retreated.

Thwack.

Thwack.

Thwack.

The sting of his spank burned like fire all over her ass. She couldn't feel or sense anything but the fuel inside her finding more and more flames to turn her to ash.

Thwack.

She pushed back as his hand found the next spot to burn.

Thwack.

Another rocking of her hips back and everything changed. The fire turned to desire. Her pussy came alive. Demanding his presence. Squeezing nothing. Needing his cock to stoke the embers.

Thwack.

She moaned hard and long.

A harsh tug.

She cried out as the clamp released and blood surged to her clit.

He thrust and she blew apart into bliss. She floated away in peace and happiness. Her body shuddered and milked his cock without even trying. Limp. Relaxed. Sated. She continued swaying with the waves of subspace until he called her back.

"Kitten," he said. "You surrendered beautifully."

"Mmm," she whispered.

He carefully untied her. With sweet, gentle caresses he glided a soapy washcloth over her, then rinsed her with a damp towel. "I love you."

"That's a wrap for today," Evan said. "Jacob, go get dressed and I'll meet you for your exit interview. Sophia, you do the same." He helped Sophia up.

She blinked and wobbled. "Wow. That was…I don't even know."

"It was a scene that will make the Best of Pussy Pleasures films." Evan walked her to her private dressing room. A cameraman followed them in.

"Ready?" Evan asked.

She inhaled. *I can do this. Nothing more for two months.* "Ready." She shimmied and smiled at the camera.

"How does it feel to be a woman?" Evan asked.

"Better than I imagined." She bit her bottom lip and smiled. "I need your prayers and positive thoughts for a healthy pregnancy." She crossed her fingers and held them up. "Help me out and send likes and comments on the stream. Let me know you want a baby for me and my billionaire lover as much as we do."

Evan took her hand, lifted it high in the air. She walked around in a tight circle so the viewers could see all of her.

She blew an air kiss. "I love all of you. Thank you for watching and giving me this opportunity to be a part of the Pussy Pleasures family."

"And you're done," Evan said. "You did a fantastic job. It was everything we asked you to do and more."

"Thanks. Is there anything else?" *I have to get*

out of here.

"How do you want to get home?" Evan asked. "Jacob or our services?"

She took the silk robe she arrived in off the hanger and wrapped it around her. *I don't know.* "Was the ceremony for real?"

"I don't know what you signed and what you didn't. It could be, but I don't know," Evan said. "I'll call legal about it, but they won't be in until Monday morning."

"I'd like to have a driver, not Jacob," she said. *I need to talk to Angie. I can't go home. I can't stay at Jacob's. If I'm married to him and my contract allows me to go home with him, I will. But until I know without a doubt that we're married and the contract states I can live with him, then I'm not living, seeing, or doing anything else with him. I'm not breaking any rules or I'll lose my bakery.*

Some of her confidence failed. *I might have just married the one man who doesn't follow rules. Most of my contract is pursuant on him following the rules laid out. If he doesn't stick to the terms of the Pussy Pleasures contract, I'll lose my bakery and my life's savings. I'll lose everything I've worked so hard for. My business partner will hate me. I might have just screwed myself.*

CHAPTER FOUR

———◆———

JACOB

SITTING IN HIS SPORTS CAR outside Zane Winslow's home, Jacob fumed. He could see Sophia standing next to Angie through the front window.

How do I get around the damn rules of the contract? Sophia, why did you get into Pussy Pleasures' company car and come here? You should have gone home with me. Me. Your husband.

He called Zane.

"Hey, buddy," Zane answered. "It's pretty late. What's up?"

"You know what's up. I want my wife escorted to my car outside your home, now."

Zane huffed and then grunted. "I'm not sure that is the wisest decision at the moment."

"Is that Jacob?" Sophia asked in the background. "Oh, God. It is. Shit."

"Maybe he should come inside," Zane said.

"Yes," Angie said. She had to be really close to Zane to get that kind of voice clarity. "That prick needs to come in and explain himself."

"Excuse me?" Jacob said. "Now I'm a prick? I want my wife to come home with me. How is that being a prick?"

"I'm not sure," Zane mumbled. "I don't understand anything that has happened in the last fifteen minutes."

"Well, you should," Angie shouted. "Get out of the house, Zane. You go out there and have a talk with Mr. Big Dick Bell, or invite him in and Sophia and I will be getting real with him. Do you understand?"

"What did *I* do?" Zane asked.

"If you weren't such a jerk about dogs, she would have had us watch Rufus. This is partly your fault. You could have—"

"Angela Winslow, what happened to Sophia's dog was no one's fault but the sick son of a bitch who murdered him. Do not blame me. Do not blame Jacob. We couldn't predict something like that, and you know it. Jacob, I think you need to come inside. We need to bring some harmony to all of this discord."

How Zane kept calm with those two women was beyond Jacob.

"He spanked her on the live stream," Angie yelled. "He *spanked* her. How could you let him do that? Her ass…Damn it. He has a *huge* hand."

"Zane wasn't there, Angie," Sophia said. "He had nothing to do with this. And I liked the spa—"

"Hush, Sophia. This is between me and Zane." Angie made a growling noise.

"I'm coming in," Jacob said. "You can't handle them." *All we need is your best friend and close neighbor Lis showing up and then I'm screwed. Sophia will never come home with me.*

"Yeah, I could use some backup," Zane said.

"I'm not giving you backup. I want to know who the other guy you had waiting for Sophia is. I want a name." Jacob ended the call. *And I'm taking my wife home.*

As he arrived at the door, he heard the Texas drawl he did not want to hear.

"Jacob Bell, you are in deep shit," Lis Greystoke shouted.

Fabulous. Hormonal Kitten 42 has arrived.

Jacob turned toward her voice. *Fuck.*

Lis and Blake Greystoke sat in the front of a souped-up pink golf cart with their dog, Bash, sitting attentively in the back seat behind Lis.

Sophia does not need to see a happy pregnant couple with their protective black lab puppy. Not today. Not. Fucking. Today. He smiled and waved. He did not want to get into it with Lis. "Good to see you too, Lis."

At least Blake rolled his eyes and mouthed *sorry.*

Lis seemed to have her foot on the accelerator as they drove over Zane's perfectly manicured front lawn.

Three guys in a room with two crazy hormonal pregnant women and one potentially pregnant or ovulating woman could make for a clusterfuck of epic proportions. Add the protective puppy into the mix and that Sophia lost her dog in a brutal…

Jacob had a bad, bad feeling Sophia wasn't going home with him and she might never go home with him.

The right side of the beautifully crafted front

doors opened.

Wearing black lounge pants, Zane pulled Jacob inside. "I have no idea what is going on. Sophia came over and Angie took her into the room with the puppies and they came out sobbing uncontrollably. The sobbing turned to screaming. Now, Angie is shouting, and Sophia is in the sniffling stage of ugly crying, again. I called Lis for reinforcements, but she didn't answer. I think she might have been on a conference call with the girls, because she texted me telling me I was one big motherfucker, and she was coming over to set things straight."

Jacob passed by Zane on his way to Sophia. "Dude, wear a shirt around my wife. And whatever you did to piss off *your* wife for makeup sex backfired. Big time. This is your doing." *You get Angie riled up all the time for sex. That's why you're about to have three kids under three.*

"Not this time. Angie and I were on track for an early bedtime." Zane followed him out of the foyer. "And this is my house. I'll wear whatever I want, whenever I want."

They arrived in the living room where the girls had been yelling, but had recently vacated.

"Where are they?" Jacob asked.

"I don't know," Zane said. "And this has to do with you. Not me."

Jacob brushed off Zane's comments. It was Sophia who submitted her name to Pussy Pleasures. Angie probably encouraged her to. "Who was the other guy waiting?"

"Someone I know who is in love with her. He's upset, but Sophia is yours. This was the only way to keep him out of the equation. He wasn't going to wait any longer, and you weren't going to act without my show forcing you to."

"Does she know him well?" *Does she have feelings for this other guy?*

Zane nodded. "Yes. Very."

Jacob racked his brain for a man with billionaire status, enough to get on the show, and to whom Sophia would have access. No one came to mind. "Is he going to try to take her from me?"

Zane shrugged. "He might. He's a good guy, honest. He might not. Depends on her and you. Stick to the rules and he won't get into the mix. Fuck up and break them, and he might get an opening."

"She's married to me." Zane's blood pressure skyrocketed. "Who does he think he is?"

Zane sighed. "Jacob, he's a lot like you and me and Blake and the rest of us good guys. If he sees she's happy with you, he'll back away and she'll never know how much he loves her. He'll find someone new. But, if he thinks for an instant that she isn't happy with you or that your marriage isn't real, he'll appear and try and take her away."

"That's never gonna happen." He walked through the living room and into the casual dining room. "Sophia," he shouted. "My lovely wife, where are you?"

"You're going to *lovely wife* her now, are you?" Angie shouted. The woman seemed on the move because her voice became louder with each word.

He followed the sound of her shrieks and found her standing in front of Sophia, guarding her. "Hi, Angie. Good to see you. I'm sorry you don't approve of spanking. I think if you watch the highlights of the show, you'll see how much Sophia did enjoy it."

Sophia's eyes looked as big as a set of sixteen-pound bowling balls when she shuddered.

There's my girl. Showing your true kinky colors.

"And I plan to do it again. Soon," Jacob stated.

Sophia rubbed her lips together.

You want me. And I'm not letting this go on any more. He offered his hand. "Sophia, we need to talk."

"Aww, hell no," Lis shouted as she stomped into the room with the tick, tick, tick of her dog's nails on the hardwood heeling beside her. "Jacob, go home. Sophia is staying with me and Blake for the time being. When you have a marriage certificate and can prove you and Sophia are married, then, and only then, will Sophia talk with you. There are rules, Jacob. Rules you're fucking up for her. Rules that have not been broken yet. Rules you need to abide by."

So Zane told you about his ownership of Pussy Pleasures. Did he tell you I'm the silent partner? I'm not being silent much longer. "Well, fuck the rules."

Pretty little Lis wearing a black dress that highlighted her belly bump shoved him aside and stood in front of Angie. "Nope. Not today. Today, we follow the rules." She cocked her head to the side and waved as she said, "Bye-bye."

"Jacob," Blake whispered. "Go home. I'll make sure the girls are taken care of tonight." He patted Jacob on the back and lowered his chin. "Stop by tomorrow night to pick something up," he mumbled. "It's the only way around the rules, and you know who set up all this bullshit, so don't give him the satisfaction." He sauntered over to Lis. "Babe, are you ready to go home?"

Lis glared at Jacob and then glanced over her shoulder at Sophia. "Ready?"

"Uh, yes," Sophia said. She glanced at Jacob.

Lis, Angie, and Sophia walked in a line past him.

Snatching Sophia from their girl chain proved easy due to their slow pace. Jacob dipped her back and crushed his mouth to hers.

She softened in his arms and parted her lips.

He moaned as he stroked along her tongue.

She wrapped her right leg around his left. A gentle *uhn* rolled from her lips into his mouth. She curled her arms around his neck and pressed her chest against his.

He cradled her back as she surrendered in his arms. "I love you," he whispered. He kissed the corners of her mouth, her cheeks, her nose, her chin, and down her neck. "Come home with me."

Lis and Angie ripped her from his arms. "No. You broke the rules."

Jacob stared into Sophia's blue eyes. "You are worth it." *I'll spend whatever it takes in fines to Pussy Pleasures in order to have you with me.*

The woman he loved lowered her chin, but a sweet, pink blush spread across her beautiful face.

"You're not the only one in this, Jacob," Lis said. "Think of her. You don't know what it would cost *her* to break the rules."

"She won't break the rules. *I will*," he said.

Lis frowned. "I don't think you're listening

to me. *You* don't know what it would cost *her* if any rules were to be broken." She glanced over her shoulder to where Zane stood seemingly like a wall barring the exit. "Zane, Sophia and I are leaving. Please walk us out."

"What about me?" Blake asked.

Lis snapped at him. "Jacob is driving you home." She poked his chest with her index finger. "You better make him understand what I said, or no sex for a month."

He closed his hand around hers and brought it to his lips. "I love you." He kissed the tip of her fingers. "You're not giving him enough credit."

"Aww," Sophia exhaled. "Don't fight over this. Jacob can drive me—"

Lis jerked her hand from Blake's and pointed at Sophia. "No." She flicked her wrist and grabbed Sophia's arm. "You are coming with me. Now." She stomped across the hardwood, tugging Sophia along with her as Bash kept pace at their side.

"Zane," Lis said in a threatening tone. "Walk. Us. Out."

"Fuck," Zane grunted. "Sophia can stay with us."

Lis spun around like a fiery tornado and got up in Zane's face. "I. Don't. Think. So."

"You tell him, Lis," Angie chimed in.

"Don't be mean to Zane," Sophia said. "It's not his fault."

"Thank you, Sophia," Zane said.

Lis huffed and pivoted, taking Sophia with her. "We're leaving. Now." She stomped away and slammed the front door.

"Thanks, Zane. Thanks a fucking lot," Blake

said. "You should have just sent them to a hotel room to get it on, not add them to your revenue stream. Sophia has no clue it's you in charge of all of this. Now you brought my wife into it, *again*." He passed Zane. "Come on, Jacob. I have to talk to you without talking to you. I'm sure you're bugged. Zane doesn't learn his lessons quickly or easily."

"Blake, you have nothing to complain about. You got everything you ever wanted because of me," Zane said. "Jacob will too. He needs to play by the rules. Remind him of the rules."

"He will be reminded," Blake stated. "He will also have his clothes burned and his house debugged," Blake said. "And, if you so much as fuck with her bakery, Angie and Lis will tear your ass up."

"Yes, we will," Angie said. "You tell him, Blake."

"What bakery?" Jacob asked. He knew Sophia baked like a dessert goddess but hadn't heard anything about a job at a bakery. *Did she quit to manage a cupcake shop? Why would she work for minimum wage? Why wouldn't she tell me?*

"She is opening a bakery," Blake said. "It's next to the coffee shop we all go to. I thought you helped her with the contract."

"I helped her with the contract," Angie said. "But she negotiated and got it at a steal."

"She's leasing the building?" *I would have bought her one in a better location.*

"Bought the building…" Angie talked about Sophia's plans as she walked into the living room. "I predict she'll have a renovation budget within the first year and have the place paid off in three." She sat on the ice-blue velvet sofa and put her legs up on the ottoman. "So, when is she getting her puppy? She's always had a dog. She needs one in her life. Did your secret love mating between Mistress Bark and Rufus produce any offspring?"

"How do you know about that?" Jacob glared at Zane. "Did you tell her?"

"You didn't sneak a mating between them without Sophia's permission?" Blake asked incredulously. "You did. You are so damn lucky. If Rufus were alive, you'd have one serious pissed off woman on your hands."

"It didn't work. Mistress Bark can't have babies. I'm going to have to find a puppy who has a heart for her like Rufus." Jacob stared at Angie. "I could use some help finding one from the dog rescue guru."

"I'll see what I can do," Angie said. Her gaze drifted to his right and her eyes narrowed and her face tightened into that of a challenge.

"Don't give me that look," Zane said. "You are out of the puppy rescuing business forever. Jacob is on his own."

"I know a guy," Blake said.

"That is not a phrase I want to hear from you after the last mess you got me into," Jacob said.

Blake patted him on the back. "Trust me on this one." He walked to the front door.

Jacob followed. "Famous last words."

As soon as they got in and closed the doors to the car, Blake took a paper and pen from his sweat jacket pocket. After writing, he ripped off the piece of paper from the small notepad and handed it to him.

You have spyware sewn into your clothes. When we get to my house, you're changing and we're burning those clothes before we talk about what went on in there. Lis is doing something similar with Sophia, only we're keeping her robe so we can have Zane hear what we want him to hear.

"So, you and Sophia got married?" Blake said.

"Yes. I'll have an announcement party in a few weeks, but first I need to have Sophia move in with me." *What kind of contracts did Blake and Lis have? Mine is a joke. I might lose a few thousand. Nothing to lose sleep over.*

Blake began writing. "Sounds good. I hope Lis and I get an invite."

You and I aren't even good friends. We're connected through Zane. We don't do anything together without Zane. And your wife is a loud piece of work.

"We'll see." He drove slowly down the street toward Blake's house. He'd never been inside the man's house. Never been invited. They always met at Zane's to talk business or travel or help them out of whatever dumbass situation the two got in. Zane was the mutual friend—not Blake, not him.

Blake held out the paper for Jacob to read.

Sophia will lose her bakery and her name will be blasted all over the internet. She will pay fines— money she doesn't have. The payment has to be her cash. You can't pay it for her and neither can her friends. There are more rules, but that gives you an idea about the severity of the situation she's in. Angie read the contracts Sophia signed as the show started. She is having a cow over it.

That's crazy. "Tell me about the man with the dog." *I better keep our conversation about nothing.*

His phone vibrated. He pulled it out of his suit jacket. *Pussy Pleasures.* He answered.

"Mr. Bell, you broke three rules. I need you to log into your account and pay your fines within an hour, per your contract," a woman said.

"I sure will. I plan on breaking the kissing rule again. So, just add that one onto the fees," Jacob said.

"I'll do that," she said. "Remember, you can only break six rules before the clause goes into effect."

"There are no clauses in my contract," Jacob said.

"There is one," she said.

Nope. I didn't sign any clauses. "What clause is that?"

"Since you married her during the live-stream, the marriage clause goes into effect. If you break six rules, we allow the second lover to pursue her and the marriage certificate will be in question," she said.

"I didn't sign anything like that," he argued.

"It was in the marriage paperwork. You signed all of it."

His phone vibrated.

"It's in the PDF I just texted you," she said. "Read it over at your convenience. Do you still want me to add the fee for a fourth blatant breaking of the rules?"

He opened the PDF and stared at the highlighted

fine print he had initialed. It hadn't been highlighted when he signed the damn thing, and he had been too damn arrogant to believe there would ever be anyone else.

Blake leaned over and read the clause. His jaw dropped.

Jacob turned left and continued driving slower than a sloth down the road. *Fuck me. Zane, you think of everything. Absofuckinglutely everything.* "No, ma'am. I'll pay what I owe right now."

"I thought so," she said. "Remember, there are eyes and ears everywhere. She has to willingly go home with you before your rules change."

"Yeah, I bet she's not allowed to do that, is she?" *I am combing through my contract when I get home.*

"I am not at liberty to discuss your wife's contract with you and neither is she," she said. "Have a good day." She ended the call.

He parked in Blake's driveway and paid his fines to Pussy Pleasures over their private app.

"Come on in and have a beer with me," Blake said. "I've got some extra clothes for you."

Jacob couldn't be sure, but he sensed some compassion in Blake's blue eyes. *What kind of hoops did Zane put you through?* "I could use a beer and a change of clothes."

Blake exited the car.

The front door opened.

Lis stood waving them inside with one hand and her finger over her lips with the other.

They walked toward the house as Jacob tried to think of all the rules of conduct in the contract. Three more mistakes and the woman he loved could be taken away. He wouldn't allow the show to force Sophia into a divorce or annulment. He wanted forever with Sophia. Blake seemed to be on his side, but Zane? How could Zane do this to him? They'd been best friends since kindergarten. He'd helped Zane fund Pussy Pleasures and stayed out of the day-to-day operations and contracts. He helped Zane keep it all from Lis, Zane's girl-bestie. Hell, he promoted the damn show in his male strip clubs.

"What are you planning on doing with your latest acquisition?" Blake asked.

Latest acquisition? The automobile dealership or the steakhouse or the racecar? Racecar. Blake loves racing. "I'm stoked. The driver is amazing and the best part is the asshole who used to own it lost it to me in a poker match. Dumbass. Never give up something that means that much to you on a game of chance. Some people are just stupid."

"When Zane told me about you being the new owner, I couldn't believe it. It was your lucky day." Blake kissed Lis on the forehead and held the door for him. Lis nodded toward the living room.

"It sure was. The driver was pissed until I got to talking with him. Now he's excited. The sponsors are thrilled. Did you see the race last week?" He followed Lis through the house and up the stairs past Blake's office and into a guest bedroom.

"I saw the race. Your guy placed third. Pretty good driving." Blake opened the top drawer of the white-washed, six-drawer dresser. "Hang out a while. You can wear these. If we drink too much, you can stay here for the night." He turned around and placed the clothes on the white-and-pink flowered comforter on the white sleigh bed. "I'll meet you in my office. I have a deal I need to talk to you about." He pointed to the oversize plastic bag and then to Jacob. Then he made the blow-up gesture with his hands.

Jacob nodded. "Okay. I'll see you in a minute."

Lis and Blake left the room and closed the door.

I'm not sure I want to know what Zane did to you and Lis, if you're going to this extreme to help me. It must have been bad.

CHAPTER FIVE

———

SOPHIA

SOPHIA'S HEAD SPUN AFTER SPEAKING to the unnamed woman from Pussy Pleasures about her breaking a rule. She paid the small fine, but needed to get to her laptop to reread the entire contract. A couple more mistakes, and she'd lose her investment in the bakery. Her business partner would have a new partner. She'd have to work as a salaried employee, not as a half-owner. She'd lose all the money she'd sunk into the place. Breaking another rule was not an option. She hadn't realized she'd broken the one she had by crying to Angie. She had no idea how they knew she'd done that until Lis. *Thank God for Lis.*

She slipped out of her robe and placed it on the hook in the guest bathroom on the first floor. She glided the wedding and engagement rings off her finger and slid them onto the ring holder next to the tray of individual hand soaps in the shape of assorted flowers. Some ibuprofen and a bottle of water stood beckoning her from the other side of the counter. A small pile of folded clothes sat on the vanity chair.

The show's attorneys had told her that they would be listening to and watching everything she did, and that it was imperative they do so to keep the show's integrity and privacy. The only person she talked to about the show was Angie. Sure, Angie would tell Zane, but the gossip train stopped there. Now she couldn't talk to Angie about her feelings for Jacob or the show or anything for two entire months. She had to keep her distance from Jacob, or she'd lose more money and her future dreams. No living with him. No sex. *If I really am married, I should be able to live with him. That is just crazy. Maybe he doesn't want me to live with him. Maybe he wants an annulment. Maybe he made some deal with the show to raise ratings with a marriage and annulment. Maybe this was all a ruse for me to be the bad kitten. I could end up being made an example of. I am not screwing my future. Jacob can do whatever the heck he wants. He has the means to handle it. I'm not losing the one thing that I have left in my life. My bakery.*

Suddenly, dressing seemed like a hardship. She pulled the light blue T-shirt dress over her head and arms and let it cascade down over her curves to mid-thigh. *Why didn't you just ask me out, Jacob? Why didn't you make a move on me? Why did it take me going on Pussy Pleasures? Why did Rufus have to die before you...What am I going to do without both of you?*

Blowing out a deep exhale slowed down the train wreck of thoughts chugging through her brain. She picked up her phone. It was an ungodly hour, but some options left little choice. She dialed her partner.

Ring.

Ring.

Ring.

"Sophia?" Hudson answered. His Texas drawl seemed clear, awake, and steady.

"I'm sorry to call you so late," she said.

"It's okay. I just got home. What's going on?"

This is it. I have to ask. I have to get out of here tonight. I don't want to talk to Lis or Blake or Jacob or even Angie. I can't chance breaking a rule. "I need a place to stay and a ride. I would never ask under normal circumstances, but I'm in a bind and this guy…Rufus is dead." She couldn't control her emotions anymore and it all came out in an ugly crying mess. "I'm…at…a friend's house. I don't want to stay here. I—"

"Text me the address. Hang on, sweetie. I'm coming."

Between wiping her eyes and failing at getting her crying under control, she texted him the address.

"I'll be there in ten. I'm so sorry. I saw something on the news about a man arrested in conjunction with a burglary and animal murder. Was that about you?"

Her voice hitched as she tried to speak and breathe. A strangled, squeaking sob came out.

"Oh, God, Sophia. You'll get through this. I promise you will."

The sound of his car accelerating eased some of her fear of losing everything.

"Stay on the phone with me," she whimpered. "I'll come out as soon as you arrive."

"I'll protect you, sweetie. I'll help you through this. You can cry to me. Let it out."

With his encouragement, she let the loss and violation that Kellen had inflicted on her, her dog, and her life pour out of her. She lost track of time as she mourned and grieved over all that she'd lost in the last twenty-four hours.

"I'm here, behind the sports car," Hudson said. "Come on."

She kept her head down as she walked out of the room.

"Ready to talk?" Lis asked.

Sophia shook her head. "I made a call. I have a friend waiting outside. I'll…Thank you for having me and giving me something to wear."

"Anytime. If there is anything I can do, please ask," Lis whispered.

"I won't be talking to anyone about anything." Sophia lowered her chin a little more. "Come to the bakery. I'll make a special cupcake just for you."

"Want a hug?" Lis held out her arms.

Sophia shook her head. "I can't. I just can't." She ran out of the house and climbed into Hudson's big, black truck.

The truck rolled forward and slowly accelerated as she stared at her hands folded in her lap. Barely dressed. No undergarments. She didn't even want to think about how ugly she had to look after crying so hard for so long.

His big hand landed softly on her thigh. "I've got a room that is yours for as long as you need or want it. No questions asked. If you need a car to drive, I've got you covered."

She gazed over at him without making eye contact. "Thank you. I'm going to have to take you up on that room. I can't go back to my…" She lifted her chin and stared up at the beige ceiling of the cab. "I can't go back there. I shouldn't have, but I went home when I found out about my dog. I went there and saw the blood." She labored to inhale. "I have to get out of the lease. I have to. I wish I hadn't gone there. I should have listened to Jacob, but I had to see for myself. There were pools of blood and splatters on the wall. What he did to my—"

"Give me names and numbers of who I need to contact, and I'll take care of it. Give me a list of what you need. I'll get my guys to handle the clean up and move. We'll store what you don't need at one of my facilities." He gently squeezed her thigh. "You're going to get through this. It's not going to be easy, but you're one strong-willed little lady and I believe you're gonna come out of this even stronger than you ever thought possible."

She lowered her gaze to his. She'd never noticed how handsome he was. Chocolate brown eyes as sweet as his Texas drawl. Chiseled cheekbones. Strong jaw. A nose that drew her eyes down to his lips…lips of a man who knew the feel of a woman's mouth on his.

She swallowed. Hard. She tried to keep focus on his face, but the muscles of his neck called to her. She loved a strong neck. A neck of a man who knew hard physical labor. Her gaze had a mind of its own as more of him came into view. Bare chest with a colored tattoo of the Texas flag. Rock-hard muscles over rock-hard muscles.

The calluses on his hands didn't register until he rubbed her thigh.

The man had on a pair of blue-and-white athletic shorts that left nothing to the imagination. He was hung. Probably as big as or bigger than Jacob.

Her heart pumped faster and faster. Her breathing…she couldn't control her sudden feelings for the man who, before that moment, she'd only seen in business suits or western wear, boots, and a cowboy hat.

He turned onto a deserted road. A gigantic gate in the shape of the state of Texas appeared between two aisles of towering cactus plants.

He tapped a remote and the gate opened. "This is my home away from home."

Her eyes had to have bugged out. The biggest house she'd ever seen stood in the distance like an oasis. Barns, buildings, horse pastures, covered riding arenas with beautiful green grass Zane would kill for expanded as far as her eyes could see.

He pointed out the different areas of the property as if it were a small piece of land and what to expect while she lived there as if she were a permanent resident.

He parked on the right side of the drive, not in the garage. "Is your car somewhere you don't want to go? I can get one of my guys to pick it up for you."

Awestruck at her surroundings, she mumbled, "That would be great. I left it at Zane and Angie Winslow's place."

"I know Zane. I'll give him a call once the sun rises and take care of that." He climbed out of his truck and while she stared at the three-level pool and pool house, he walked around and opened her door.

Without asking, he slid his hands under her thighs and behind her back. He carried her from the car into his magnificent home. "It's been a long time since a lady lived with me."

"I'll try to stay out of your way," she said, but the husky voice that came from her lips surprised her.

"Naw, sweetheart," he said. "It'll be nice having you here. Get in my way as much as possible." He adjusted her in his arms and walked into an enormous master suite with a lone star made of horseshoes welded together and hung above the dark-brown leather headboard.

He placed her on the soft, blue duvet covering the mattress. "Do you want to be alone? Or snuggle with a friend? Nothing but comfort. I promise to be an absolute gentleman. My momma would kill me if I behaved inappropriately. And the last thing I'd ever do is piss off my momma or take advantage of a pretty lady who got her world ripped out from under her."

She did something she never in a million years would have ever done—she took his hand and turned down the covers. She didn't speak, just held his hand as he joined her in bed.

"Don't you worry about a thing," he whispered. "You're safe with me."

She closed her eyes and scooted backward until her back was flush against his front. "Thank you, Hudson. I didn't know who else to call."

"I'm glad you called me."

And she was glad to be in the arms of a gentleman, even though she wished she could be in Jacob's arms, wished she could believe her Pussy Pleasures lover truly was her husband. She'd tackle the rest of her problems tomorrow. Tonight, she was safe from Kellen, safe from the watchful eyes of Pussy Pleasures, safe from breaking the rules with the man she wasn't sure if she had truly married or not.

CHAPTER SIX

JACOB

WAITING TO HEAR FROM SOPHIA did not work for Jacob Bell. He had no idea where she was staying and neither did Lis or Blake or Angie. Zane knew but wasn't telling and because Jacob was the Billionaire 43, he had been locked out of all access to those records. Someone else cleaned Sophia's apartment, paid off her lease, and moved her belongings to whereabouts unknown before he made the first phone call.

Standing in line like everyone else for Sophia's bakery to open, Jacob berated himself for not camping out in front of the bakery last night. He'd gotten there an hour early, but not early enough to be first in line. Where he stood at the corner of the street, he'd be lucky to step foot inside the establishment within an hour.

Blake walked by him and stopped. He turned around. "Why are you here?"

"I want to see Sophia," Jacob said.

"Really? I'm not an idiot," Blake said. "I mean, why aren't you inside already?"

Jacob looked around and gestured to the line of people in front and behind him. "I'm waiting in line like everyone else until the store opens. I don't want to be banned from the bakery before it ever opens."

"Dude, come with me," Blake said. "Lis is inside getting a special order for our employees at the club. I need help carrying."

This is my lucky day. "Lead the way." *Are you wearing a wire? Should I ask you again about Sophia's living arrangements? Would it be worth breaking another rule?*

"How was your weekend?" Blake asked.

"It sucked," Jacob said. "Yours?"

Blake looked at him for a second. "It did?"

"Yeah. I have no idea where Sophia is staying. She won't answer my calls. She won't text me back. Her apartment was cleaned and emptied and the contents moved somewhere I am not allowed access to or information about. I had the wedding and engagement rings she left at your house checked for any spyware. There was none, but I had to be sure. I brought them with me. I don't know what I'll do if she refuses them."

His phone vibrated. He took it from his suit jacket, and lo and behold, Pussy Pleasures was calling him. *Fuck.*

He answered the call.

"Mr. Bell, you broke four more rules. The marriage is in serious jeopardy, and the first of the marriage clauses is now enacted. I hope for your sake that your Kitten 43 loves you enough to keep from breaking her contract rules with us. You have an hour to pay your fines. I hope this is the last time I speak with you. The next time, all the clauses will be enforced and not only will your fines increase, but your marriage license and certificate will also be in jeopardy."

He hung up, and pulled up the app and paid his fines. "You're in on this, aren't you?"

"I don't know what you're talking about," Blake said. "I'm not in on anything except getting these cupcakes for my employees."

"I fucking hate Zane. If Angie weren't having such a difficult pregnancy, I'd beat the fuck out of him for what he's putting me through."

Blake opened the door to the—

Jacob couldn't breathe. He couldn't move. His Sophia smiled as she tucked a cupcake into a single box that was stacked on top of five dozen cupcake boxes. The image of her in his home with nothing but that blue-and-white apron with *Sophia's Sweets* printed in hot pink on the front made his body jerk. *Mine.*

He left Blake in his dust as he strode toward her.

Behind the glass separating the front from the kitchen stood his lovely wife. She paid no attention to anyone as she walked to the front with the stack of white boxes in her hands. Her head hung low.

Have you been losing sleep over me? I've been a mess without you.

She carefully placed the boxes on the counter at checkout, next to the display of beautifully decorated cupcakes, cookies, and pastries. Her head rose and unsure blue eyes gazed into his. She lifted the small, white box on top and placed it beside the stacked boxes.

Blake picked up the stack of boxes. "Thanks,

Sophia. Did Lis leave through the back?"

"You can leave through there too. The door locks automatically," Sophia said. "So all you have to do is make sure it's closed."

"Gotcha," Blake said. He nudged Jacob with his elbow. "See you soon."

"Yeah," Jacob said. *Probably won't. I'm so angry with Zane, I'm avoiding that section of the neighborhood for a while.*

"For you." She slid the single cupcake box forward.

He took the black velvet box from his jacket's inner pocket and placed it on the counter. "These are yours." He slid the box toward her.

"I can't. I recently received a call stating…well, I just can't." She pushed the box with the rings that should be showing everyone she was his wife back toward him.

He picked up the jewelry box with his left hand, showing her that he wore his wedding band. "Can you keep it until—" He stopped from blurting out about the show, but the silence between them ate away at his heart. He reached across the counter and cradled the back of her head. "I love you. No matter what you hear or see or feel, I love you and only you. There is no one else in my life. No one else who will ever share my bed, my body, my life. Only you. Forever you."

"Jacob." Pressing her fingers to her lips, she stopped speaking. She squeezed her lids shut and shook her head. "Don't do this."

"You tell me all the time to calm down, to cool off, to—"

"Jacob, please. I can't. You don't understand

what will happen."

He leaned forward and kissed her lips. "Make me a cupcake every morning. Whatever you're in the mood to give me. I'll be here, in line, waiting to see you." He slipped the velvet box into the pocket of her apron. "I love you."

His phone vibrated. *Fuck.* "What do I owe you?"

"Nothing," she whispered. She glanced down. "Don't eat the cookie at the bottom. That's for Mistress Bark. It's dog friendly." She stepped backward, making him release his gentle hold.

The whining sounds of a puppy seemed to call him to turn around.

A man about Jacob's height and build wearing a dark brown business suit, cowboy boots, and a brown Stetson walked in holding a gray-and-black Pitbull mix in his arms. "He's scrubbed clean and got his shots. Anything else you can think of that the little guy needs, sugar?" He stood a short distance from the display and Jacob.

Her eyes lit up the room with joy. She smiled that smile she used to give Rufus when he played with Mistress Bark. "Is he for me?"

The man Jacob had never set eyes on until that moment took off his hat and nodded. "Yes, ma'am. I saw him and thought of you. I wanted to introduce you two and see if you fell for him the way I did."

She hustled around the counter and passed Jacob. The ease with which she took the puppy from the man's arms worried Jacob. They were close, possibly hovering on more-than-friends close.

Who is this guy? Jacob smiled and held out his

hand. "I'm Jacob Bell. Sophia is my—"

"Jacob used to be my boss," she interjected.

The man greeted him like a friend with a firm handshake. "Nice to meet you, Jacob. I'm Sophia's business partner, Hudson Fox. I'm glad you came in. Did you give him that cupcake and cookie for Mistress Bark?"

How do you know about my dog and yet I don't know anything about you?

Rubbing her face against the sweet puppy's forehead, Sophia cooed something.

"She gave them to me," Jacob said. *You don't look like a baker. Sophia never mentioned you. Never mentioned a partner. Never mentioned fucking any of this.*

Hudson nodded toward the dining area off to the side. "I've got a few minutes before I take that pup away from her for the day." He walked past Sophia. "He's not staying today. We've got to get him a crate and some toys. I'll have one of my guys swing by with an inspector to see what renovations we might have to make to accommodate a guard dog for the front of the bakery. We'll do whatever it takes to keep you safe when you're here alone."

She nodded and continued cuddling the pup.

Jacob stopped and kissed Sophia's cheek. "He's cute. Why don't you bring him home tonight?"

She barely made eye contact. "Stop. I can't see you. Not like that. Not alone. Not at your house. Not where I'm staying. No invitations. Nothing."

He wrapped his arm around her waist and felt both his phone and hers vibrate. *I did it again. Damn it.*

She squirmed out of his side hug and over to

Hudson. "I have to take this call." She handed the puppy to the big guy. "Are you stopping by later?"

"Yes, ma'am. My mom is flying in from Austin to experience our bakery for herself. She's a handful, but she's gonna love this place. Good luck with your call. Let me know if you need anything."

"Thank you." Sophia tapped her phone and hurried to the back, her shoulders slouched and her head dropped forward in utter defeat.

"She's worked so hard for this," Hudson said. "The girl is running on empty." He turned to Jacob. "I called my mom to come help. I don't know the first thing about baking. I can grill damn near anything, but I can't bake worth a damn." He shook his head and pressed his lips together. "She's lost her sass. Losing her dog the way she did took its toll on her. I don't know what else happened this weekend, but the girl is a bundle of nerves everywhere else but here. I'm about to tear into whoever keeps calling her." He turned and looked at Jacob. "Do you know what's going on?"

"It's complicated," Jacob said. *You are not involved with Pussy Pleasures. She is not into you. Not at all. And you don't seem into her. Not like I am.* "I'll see what I can find out about those phone calls." His phone continued to buzz in his pocket. *I'm going to find a loophole in the contract. I've got to talk to Zane and find out who the other man is who can now pursue my Sophia.* "I'll swing by this afternoon to check on her."

Hudson shook Jacob's hand. "Then I'll see you later. It's been great to put a face with a name."

Wish I could say the same to you. Jacob pivoted, taking one last look at his wife who had her head high and her back straight again. He expected Hudson to follow his lead, but the man waved at Sophia.

"Ten minutes before the doors open. You ready, sweetheart?" Hudson asked.

Sweetheart? Is that a southern thing? Or are you interested in my wife?

She strode out like she had something to prove. "I am so ready. Blake and Lis have their cupcakes loaded. I've got cupcakes marked and ready in the back for those online orders. Tell your mom that I can't wait to meet her and to be prepared to bake." She grinned, and although it didn't reach her eyes, she faked it well enough for anyone else to believe life had never been better.

"That's the business partner who is gonna burn it up in sales. Actually, that might not be the best choice of words."

Sophia laughed. "No burning, Hudson. None."

"Good luck today. The line is wrapped around the block. Get a new apron on. That one has this pup's fur all over it."

She laughed. "Best present ever. Thank you so much, Hudson." She blew him a kiss.

He reached up and caught it in his hand as if it were real. "Loving that sugar, little lady."

"That was for the pup, not you," she teased. "Give it to him. He wants it."

"Nope, I'm keeping that one." Hudson walked out, leaving Jacob alone with her.

The smile she wore for Hudson vanished. "You need to go. Now."

"Why is he calling you sweetheart? Does he know you're mine? That you're married to *me?*"

"One, he's a Texan. They do things like that. Two, he doesn't know shit about us or my personal life besides the nightmare of what happened at my house and to my dog. Three, there is no proof we're married. Four, you don't have any claim to me. Period. End of story. Go away, Jacob. You're not ruining any other aspect of my life today." She shooed him.

"You are married to me. You are my wife. You better let him know you're mine. Or, *sugar,* I will. I will stake my claim so loud and clear, the entire world will know exactly who you are, Sophia Bell." His voice rose and before he knew it, he had her in his arms, dipped back. His lips crushed hers, his tongue stroking, dancing, dominating hers. "I love you. I love you, and I want the world to know how much I love my *wife.*"

His phone buzzed over and over. "Damn it." He grabbed his phone. "What?"

"You've broken more rules," the female voice of Pussy Pleasures said. "Your marriage license and certificate are put on hold. You are not married. I repeat, you are not married to Sophia. The other interested party has been notified, and he plans to pursue her with every means available at his disposal. Your arrogance got you here. Pay your fines, Jacob. And don't ignore my calls ever again."

"Fuck you," Jacob said. He looked at Sophia, still cradled in one arm. "This game that we're in—I'm going to win it for us. Whatever they have over you, I'm going to find out, and I'm going to pay for your freedom."

She parted her lips and then closed them. "Mr. Bell, you've made your point."

He pulled her up and against his chest. "I love you. Please tell me you know I love you."

"Sometimes love isn't enough," she whispered.

I'm losing you. I can't lose you. "Love is enough. Trust me in that. Love *is* enough."

She shrugged and, although she stayed in his embrace, he felt her retreat.

"It's not enough today." She left his arms. "Don't forget your cupcake." Her hand drifted over the counter, up the edge of the white box, over and down to the counter again as she walked around the glass display. She seemed to begin the mental list of things to do before opening the doors.

He took the cupcake box. One last glance at the woman he loved more than his own life, and he walked out the door.

Once inside the safety of his car, he opened the box. A small, handwritten note was taped to the inside of the lid.

I had hoped you'd come to the bakery today. I can't handle a fight right now. If you continue to pursue me, I will lose everything I've worked so hard for. I've lost so much in the last couple of days. Please, don't be the reason I lose my business.

Yours,

Sophia

P.S. I hope you like wedding cake.

He gazed down at the white cupcake with a small figurine of a man in a tux and a woman in a wedding dress and veil. "You do love me."

He heard Blake whisper as if he were in the car

with him. "*You don't know her contract. Zane scared the fuck out of Lis, which is how we got out of the punishments in both of our contracts and still got the bonus.*"

I can't leave you alone, Sophia. But I can control myself as long as no one else tries to get between us. I'll have to talk to your partner about looking out for anyone who asks you out on a date.

CHAPTER SEVEN

SOPHIA

WITH THE CLOSED SIGN HUNG on the door, Sophia took out the binder of closing procedures Hudson had written for the shop. They hadn't had time to go over closing protocol, and since he was stuck at the airport waiting on his mom's delayed flight, she planned to surprise both of them by following his instructions.

1. Take a deep breath. You made it through another busy day at Sophia's Sweets.

She inhaled and smiled. She'd sold out of all her cupcakes and pastries, and only a few cookies remained. The soft opening had surpassed her expectations. She'd need Hudson's mom's help. Deep relief that the woman Hudson bragged on whenever possible was coming to work for free to get the bakery started on the right foot made Sophia feel special and part of a family again.

One by one, she continued down the list made for someone who knew little to nothing about closing up a business for the day. Whoever she hired could follow the protocol and finish within an hour or less.

Since she had to wait for his return, she put together boxes for the following day's orders, and wrote the specials for the rest of the week on a chalkboard stand she planned to place outside in the morning.

Three raps on the back door alerted her that Hudson was there. He unlocked the door and held it open for a fifty-something brunette with dark eyes and curly hair.

"Howdy," the woman shouted and held out her arms. "Come here, baby. I need a little squeeze."

Sophia didn't know whether to laugh or cry at the bundle of exuberance greeting her. With an unsure smile and a slight hesitation, Sophia stepped forward.

The woman made an adorable hop-step, then a full-on sprint, expanding her wing-length for that hug. In less time than a quick gasp, Sophia had been wrapped up and hugged and squeezed and had her face cupped and forehead kissed like she was a long-lost daughter.

"Hudson didn't tell me you were the prettiest little thing this world has ever had the pleasure of seeing." She shrugged as if she were hugging Sophia again. "Lord did something special when he made you."

She let Sophia go and then walked around the room, flaring her long A-line skirt, showing off beautiful and expensive tan leather boots that matched her vest.

Hudson winked at Sophia. "Sorry we're so late. Mechanical troubles. Momma had Dad come out to the airport and find out what was wrong. He decided he didn't like the pilot or the mechanical team, so he took her to the private airport and flew her in one of our planes." He looked around. "Dad is waiting in the truck. You're gonna have two helpers for a couple weeks." He nodded and took off his hat. "You did good. Real good."

Mrs. Fox spun around and faced them. "Better than good. Look at this place. It's fabulous. I'm so proud of the both of you. I see franchises in your future." She rushed over to Sophia and took her hand. "Girl, grab your purse. The boys are taking us home. Tex brought fresh steaks and bacon from the ranch. We're celebrating tonight."

"Momma, you're freaking her out," Hudson said.

Mrs. Fox *tsked*. "Sweet boy, I'm doing no such thing. You don't understand the immediate bond of bakers. I'm getting our tiaras out tomorrow. That might freak her out a little, but she'll get over it quickly when she sees how beautiful we both look in sparkling diamonds from Auntie Fox's diamond mine."

"Real tiaras?" Sophia asked. *No. Not real?*

"As real as a heart attack," Mrs. Fox said. Her dark eyes beamed with an inner joy. She leaned in as if they were conspirators. "We're gonna make Tex wear one, too." Her smile was infectious.

Sophia giggled and returned the smile tenfold. "I can't wait," she whispered.

"I can tell already, you two are going to be thick as thieves within twenty-four hours," Hudson said.

Sophia grabbed her black leather purse off the hook. "Are you scared?"

"Ooooooh," Mrs. Fox said. "I think she's

challenging you."

Hudson shook his head. "Momma, Sophia is always challenging me. It's why we're business partners." He opened the back door. "Ladies, your chariot awaits."

A man the spitting image of Hudson, only about twenty-five years older, stood holding the passenger door. "Where are the cupcakes?"

"Sold out," Sophia said. "Sorry. I can bake some when we get to the house." She walked behind Mrs. Fox. As soon as Hudson's mom climbed into the truck, Sophia held out her hand to Mr. Fox.

"We're huggers, little lady," Mr. Fox said. He wrapped his arms around her and squeezed her tight. "You're as sweet as Hudson said. I'd like it if you'd bake us something for dessert tonight. It doesn't have to be a cupcake. Momma says I've got a sweet tooth, but I disagree."

Hudson saved her from another hug. He pulled her from his father and helped her into the back. "I can drive."

His father made a guttural noise. "Naw, I'm driving. I need to get the lay of the land."

Both men closed the doors and walked to the other side of the truck. She couldn't stop staring at Mr. Fox. *Hudson will look exactly like you when he's your age—gorgeous, sexy, and strong as an ox.*

The truck seemed small with both Hudson and his father in it.

As they drove away, Hudson shifted in the seat next to her. She'd never noticed how big the man's thighs were.

"Thanks for picking me up," she said.

He leaned over and whispered, "The pup is in the crate tied down in the back. We're going to have to keep him in the bedroom. My mom and dad aren't fond of inside pets, but I am. When I was a kid, I snuck my border collie into my room every night and then took him outside when I went to school. My parents turned a blind eye. They haven't visited me here, so I want them to be comfortable and give them the illusion of no pets in the house."

She turned her head and accidently brushed her lips over his before reaching his ear. A zing of electricity shot through her. She didn't mean to, but she grabbed onto his suit jacket to steady herself. A sensation of falling gripped her. She exhaled into his ear and wanted to say something, but her mind shut down. "I. Okay."

"Sweetheart, I know you're going through a rough patch right now, but I'm here for you." He turned his head as she turned hers.

They hesitated in the middle when their mouths lined up perfectly for a…

His hot lips pressed against hers. His hands… *God, your hands. You shouldn't feel this good. I wasn't expecting—*

She moaned as his tongue swept into her mouth. His callused hand slid from her cheek to the back of her neck, guiding her, pulling her in for a deeper, more thorough tasting. He shifted. He slid her onto his lap, her legs straddling his big thighs.

She squeaked a sexy noise all too unfamiliar.

He growled with a vibration that singed her girlie parts. Her back hit something hard. She opened her mouth and broke the kiss. Panting for air, she made a strange, guttural moan.

"Fuck," he mumbled. He crushed his lips to her and spun her around and down. He thrust and that big cock confined in his pants rubbed against her clit. He backed and thrust again, hard.

"Oh, God," she gasped. "I'm." She inhaled. "I—"

Doors opened and slammed closed.

The heat and weight of Hudson vanished with one strong pull. She wobbled as she found her footing on the driveway in the back of Hudson's ranch.

Tex supported her as she regained brain function. "It was getting a bit too hot for me and Momma. Figured you and my son needed a break before things got too out of hand."

"I'm not sure what happened back there." She slid her hands down the front and sides of her pink dress, pulling the hem at the back out of her black panties.

"Looked to me like a chemical explosion," Tex said. "My son doesn't show affection for the girls he dates. I've never seen him even touch one. He damn near…well, little miss, he seems to have a mighty big affection for you."

Oh, my word. We were dry humping in front of his parents. I don't do that. I don't. Embarrassment creeped up her neck and face until it consumed her. "I am so sorry. That will never happen again. I am not like that. I don't—I—I am so sorry." She lowered her gaze to her bare feet. *I must have kicked off my shoes. I'm not even going to say anything.*

"It's okay. Just apologize to Momma for

knocking her in the head with your pretty pink shoes."

Please, no. I want to die. "Yes, sir. I'm so sorry." She groaned in misery.

"Apology accepted," Tex said. "Go inside and do whatever you ladies do after a long day at work to look and smell as pretty as you do for us men."

She hurried along inside the house and straight into the bedroom. Without stopping, she rushed toward the bathroom. She should have looked up. She should have slowed down. She should have done a million other things, but didn't. She barreled into the man who opened up his wallet and his house to her.

Dazed from the direct hit to a relative brick wall of a man, she stumbled back and hit the edge of the bed so hard her legs flew up and she fell backward onto the bed.

"Oh, shit," he mumbled. "Sorry. Sorry. I wasn't paying attention." He hovered over her, his hands patting her down and then cupping the sides of her face. "Talk to me, Sophia. Are you conscious?"

She opened her eyes and seemed to get hit with a jolt of energy that could have rivaled a lightning strike. "I'm..." Her mouth was so dry, she needed water...cold, icy water. Freezing cold, arctic water. Water so cold that the fire burning inside her would extinguish in the next two seconds or she might do something she never intended on doing.

His expression softened. The worry in his brown eyes morphed to something altogether different.

I want you. I want to feel what it's like to make love to you.

"I know you're trying to work through a truckload of feelings, and I don't want to add to your list," he said, then paused. The eyes she counted on to stay steady and strong and all-business seemed to show more of the soft, tender, and loving side he'd opened up to her last night. "But, sugar, I'm going to. I know you've got feelings, strong ones, for your ex-boss. He's a good guy from what I've heard about him, and I checked him out. But he's a hothead and you need to know what it's like to be with a man who sticks to rules, remains steady in all circumstances, and can give you a life filled with children, love, and family. I'd never stifle your career, only help you to thrive within it." He kissed her lips and his voice turned into a sexy, gravelly Texas drawl. "And I want you to know what it feels like to have me inside you," he whispered. "You can't make a choice without knowing your options."

He made some very valid points. Points that she repeated over and over in her mind, especially the one about feeling him inside her. She'd never been with anyone except Jacob. She'd never expected to be interested in anyone else, but Jacob kept breaking the rules. He lied to her about being married. He lied to her about protecting her. If he had gotten down on one knee and proposed, she could be wearing the engagement and wedding rings in that pretty jewelry box he shoved in her apron. If he hadn't talked about the dang show, she wouldn't have lost the savings with which she had planned to finish renovating the second floor of the bakery. He cost her the last of her savings because she believed in him. She believed the man who bid on her wouldn't break the rules, and she was stupid enough to put that in her contract. Hell, she never in a million years expected *him* to be her lover on the show or she wouldn't have accepted all the clauses about her billionaire following all the rules. Every portion of her contract was tied to her partner. The team at Pussy Pleasures had thought of everything, added clause upon clause. She wanted a baby so desperately she didn't care about the contract or the clauses, didn't think she'd be partnered with a man like Jacob. She knew she wouldn't break any rules, and they seemed to know it, too. The addition of a financial tie to her lover's actions seemed cruel now that she knew she was matched with Jacob. Jacob broke rules. He used his finances and his brain to work the angles in business, to get ahead, to keep the people he trusted around him.

Hudson didn't have any part in that show, or her contract with them. He didn't know what she'd done, only that her heart had been broken and her life had been ripped out from under her in the last couple of days. He genuinely cared for her. She wasn't sure Jacob Bell cared enough about anyone but himself, not even the baby she might be carrying inside her.

Her phone rang loudly.

Ever the gentleman, Hudson climbed off her and handed over her purse, which had dropped on the floor.

Sitting, she answered the call in the nick of time.

"Sophia?" Jacob asked before she ever opened her mouth.

"Yeah, it's me." She gazed up at Hudson.

"Take your time," Hudson said.

She nodded and watched him take off his jacket as he walked into the bathroom suite.

"Who was that?" Jacob asked.

"Hudson."

"Oh. Are you busy tomorrow night?" Jacob asked. "I'm not breaking any rules asking."

"Did you eat the cupcake I baked you?" She didn't know what to do with herself. She loved Jacob, but she was too scared to live on her own. After going to the police department with Hudson and talking to the police officer in charge of Kellen's arrest that weekend, Hudson closed the door on staying anywhere else until the evil man was sentenced and in prison. She agreed to stay, at least until she was called back to Pussy Pleasures for the pregnancy reveal or fail with Jacob.

"Yes. It was delicious. I wish I had known you wanted a bakery. Why didn't you tell me?"

"I baked cookies and cakes and croissants and beignets at least once a week. And you never asked me what I wanted to do for the rest of my life. You never asked, Jacob. Never. Not once." *It was always me asking you questions about your life, about your dreams, about you.*

"I asked and moved you around in the company. You never said you wanted to be an entrepreneur. After all the time we spent together, at work, at my house, at dinners, and in the club, you never mentioned baking as something you wanted to pursue. Why?"

Her blood pressure rose. "I'm not arguing with you about this. I mentioned hating my job. I mentioned leaving a bazillion times. What did you think I wanted to do?"

Silence.

"Well?"

Silence.

"I guess there is nothing to talk about. Bye, Jacob." She was about to hit *End*—

"I wasn't sure. Everywhere I put you in the organization, you excelled and then threatened to quit. My mom baked. She loved it, but never wanted a bakery. She just enjoyed feeding everyone all the time. I was planning on offering you a new position in my hotel division. I didn't like you getting closer to the dancers in the club. I didn't like how open they were with you touching them. I hated it, but damn if you didn't increase the profits of that fledgling division. You turned those clubs around within three months. I couldn't believe it. I was going to cut that division loose until you took over."

"Your mom baked?" *You almost never mention your parents.*

"Yeah. She was an incredible woman. She would have loved you and you would have loved her. Would you be eating lunch or dinner tomorrow?"

She walked a fine line with him. She had to have her guard up with him around or the next mistake could mean the bakery was no longer hers. "I will be taking my lunch break around two in the afternoon tomorrow. I will be staying at the bakery and eating at the table closest to the register."

"What a coincidence. I'm taking my lunch around that time." He didn't ask her out or outright plan a date. He asked a question and she answered.

The intention was clear. He'd meet her for lunch, most likely bring her lunch.

"I have to go," she said. "Did you have a favorite dessert your mom used to bake you?"

"Mocha torte cupcakes," he said softly. "Whipped cream frosting with a hint of coffee and cocoa."

"Sounds delicious," she said. *I'll make you my version tomorrow.*

"I love you," he whispered. "So much."

She couldn't bring herself to say the words. Telling him her feelings was against the rules, anyway. No intentional contact. No intentional touching. Definitely no kissing. But they could have sex. How would that work with no intentional touching? Regardless, she wasn't breaking any more rules. None. "Maybe I'll see you around."

"It's a small city," Jacob said. "We can't help but run into each other."

"Goodnight, Jacob," she said.

"'Night, Sophia."

She ended the call and flopped back onto the bed. *I love you, Jacob. You make me crazy and then you make me love you all the more.*

CHAPTER EIGHT

Jacob

A S HE APPROACHED THE BAKERY, shivers worked up and down Jacob's spine like they did when a business negotiation was about to go bad. Something was off. She didn't answer his calls or texts that morning. He hadn't broken any of the rules since yesterday afternoon. He'd been busy with a new deal, and he hadn't had any interaction with her to get worked up enough to break any more rules. It was early, but he planned to stay calm and follow the rules of his contract.

He couldn't shake the feeling that someone had already weaseled their way into her life, but he also couldn't figure who that someone could be.

The line for the bakery seemed to grow behind him. *My girl is killing it as a bakery entrepreneur.* Even with dread filling his stomach, he remained proud of her accomplishment. *I wish I were a part of this. I wish you had asked me about being a partner or investor. Why choose a man who moved here a year ago? Why someone with no experience in the food service industry? How did you meet Hudson Fox from Austin, Texas?*

He opened the door for a woman and two toddlers, hoping this time he would be able to move inside the building.

The woman looked at him. "Thank you. She's out of the chocolate cupcakes, so you're going to have to wait twenty minutes for those."

He looked at the three boxes most likely filled with three dozen cupcakes. "Party?"

"Yes," the woman said. "The other bakery in town screwed up my order. I called over here, praying for a miracle, and God delivered. Sophia took care of me. Did you know she has a separate kitchen upstairs for nut- and seed-free baked goods? Nothing with nuts is allowed up there. Gluten free is up there too. And she gave my kids samples to choose from. I will never go anywhere else." The woman seemed to stand taller as she spoke. "You will not only love her, but you will sink your teeth into a slice of bliss with every bite." She left him with a smile, her kids in tow asking when they could eat another cupcake.

Three more people left the bakery with boxes of goodies as he held the door. He stepped inside the deliciously scented establishment and tried not to salivate.

A woman in her early fifties worked with Sophia, helping with orders, delivering goodies to tables, and checking customers out. A big, sturdy, older guy in a cowboy hat, western shirt and jeans wearing a blue-and-white apron with *Sophia's Sweets* in pink lettering brought out boxes and assisted them.

A hearty laugh filled the shop. The man took

off his hat, uncovering a thick head of light-brown hair. The face of Sophia's partner, only older, appeared from the shadows of the Stetson's brim.

Hudson's parents are here, helping Sophia.

Hudson's parents seemed to know exactly how everything worked, from the supplies to baking to customer service. Hudson had a family there to support him and Sophia. He had everything Sophia had always said she wanted—a family.

All the air left his lungs as reality hit him as hard as it had when his parents died. *Hudson is the other man—the lover who had waited at Pussy Pleasures for him to drop out. Hudson Fox is the billionaire in love with my Sophia. I can't give her what he can. It's just me. An only child of only children. And my parents passed away years ago.*

The older woman hugged Sophia and seemed to float on cloud nine as she bragged on the peanut butter and jelly cupcakes. "Wait until you try them. They are almost as good as Sophia's fabulous lemon pound cake and mocha and raspberry torte cupcakes." The woman sold the goods and Sophia at the same time. A genuine adoration for Sophia flowed through every word and gesture. Sophia had charmed the couple like she charmed everyone.

Jacob held the picnic basket she'd bought him two years ago in one hand and hoped Sophia would sense his presence and gaze his way. *I've got to make the very most of my time with you.*

He approached the display case and their eyes finally met. "Hi. Are there any more mocha tortes?"

"I've got this," the older woman said.

"Thanks, but I'll take care of him. Do you mind if I take my lunch break?" Sophia asked.

The woman's gaze fell to his and a slight drop in her big smile made his heart ache a little less. Hudson's mom wouldn't stop Sophia, and with the crowd manageable for one or two people, she didn't have an excuse for Sophia not to stop for lunch. "Sure. Is this Jacob?"

"Yes," Sophia said. "My ex-boss." She tipped her chin up and glanced at the lounging area. "Meet you over there?"

"I need a couple cupcakes," Jacob said.

"How many?" Sophia asked.

"At least two for now, but I'd like two dozen cupcakes to bring back to work." His stomach tied into knots. He had his entire future riding on keeping to Pussy Pleasures' rules for the next couple months until they returned to the studio for the pregnancy reveal or fail. Arrogance led him to this place—a place where he had to fight off heavy competition. The kind of competition he would never get involved in when it came to something or someone so special he couldn't bear to lose.

Sophia smiled and his heart skipped a beat. "Mrs. Fox, could you fix Jacob up with two dozen of our most expensive and beautifully frosted cupcakes to go?"

Jacob laughed. "Make it four dozen. I might need some help carrying them out."

Mrs. Fox rolled her eyes, but Mr. Fox expelled a hefty bark of a laugh.

"Zane Winslow told me about you," Mr. Fox said. "You're everything he said you were, and you have a sense of humor." He strode toward the counter. "I'll check him out, Sophia. You go sit down and enjoy your lunch."

"I can—" Sophia began.

"No, ma'am," Mr. Fox said. "You go on. No discounts, young lady. You have a business to run."

Sophia snuggled up to the big man and side-hugged him. "Thank you."

The man blushed. "Go on. You've been saving those two cupcakes for him. So, go get them."

Sophia didn't hesitate. She untied her pink apron and lifted it over her head. She placed it on a hook near the entrance to the kitchen.

"We've got four dozen cupcakes to go and two for dine-in," Mr. Fox said as he typed the order into the tablet.

"Yes, sir." Jacob handed him a credit card. "Add a four-thousand-dollar tip, please."

Mr. Fox's gaze lifted from the tablet screen. "Four thousand?"

"Make it twenty thousand, please," Jacob said. *I know my girl had to pay Pussy Pleasures a fine. This might help recover some of the costs.*

Mr. Fox gazed down. "That's one big tip."

"No discounts, right?" *You need to tell your son I'm not playing. He's bringing in his family to help. I'm bringing in my larger bank account.*

The man clenched his jaw. "Right." He swiped the card. "So, Jacob, what do you do?" He handed Jacob the card and receipt.

"I win, sir, or I don't play." Jacob slipped the card into his inside jacket pocket. "Thank you."

The man grunted. "Thanks for coming to

Sophia's bakery."

"Jacob," Sophia said with a nod and a wave. She lifted up two plates with cupcakes. "Dessert first?"

"Whatever you'd prefer, but you might want to wait until you see what I brought." Jacob turned toward the lounge where a few new sofas and tables sat in the far corner.

Sophia joined him on the way to the only semi-secluded area of the bakery.

Refusing the compulsion to say *the hell with the rules*, throw her over his shoulder and carry her home, Jacob placed the picnic basket down on the coffee table in front of the mint-green velvet sofa. "How has your day been?"

"Crazy busy," she said. "I don't know what I'd do without Hudson's parents helping me this week. I think they're going home after this initial opening-week rush. I've got to hire someone part time." She placed the cupcakes down. "I made two different mocha tortes. One with raspberries for the business and one classic for you."

She sat down on the couch with a big grin. "I think you're going to eat both of them. I want to know how they compare to your mom's."

Jacob opened the top of the basket and one-by-one emptied the contents. "One turkey sub with all the fixings. A veggie platter, and two bottles of water."

"You never change. We're sharing the sandwich?"

"It's huge. I have plates." He handed her silver utensils wrapped up in a cotton napkin, and then flipped the lid off the veggie platter he'd put together earlier in the day. "Your eyes are always bigger than your stomach. I have the same issue. Plus, we need to save room for an extra dessert." He lifted a small container with a slice of the mocha torte he made last night to impress her. "My mom's recipe with my less than stellar baking skills."

"You baked for me?"

The shock on her face and the way she kept shaking her head in denial cut his soul open. He hadn't taken care of her the way he should have. He'd been so damn angry at life and love that he'd neglected the one person left in his life whom he loved.

He nodded. "Yeah. Don't expect too much. It's been a long time since I made this." *Since mom and dad's funeral.*

She unrolled the utensils and placed the napkin on her lap. Instead of placing the fork, knife, and spoon down, she kept the fork in her hand and took the container out of his hand. With a quick snap of her fingers over the plastic top, the lid was off and on the table. Her fork dug down to the bottom and lifted the two layers of cake and frosting. The cake disappeared in her mouth and her hand with the fork dropped to her lap. She flopped backward against the couch. Her shoulders dropped a solid inch as she swallowed.

"Oh. My. Goodness. You can bake." She gazed at him and a sexy smiled spread over her lips. "That is sinfully delicious. You did some kind of rum and butter…" She looked at the cake container like it would give her an orgasm and then at him. "Jacob Bell, I had no idea." She closed her eyes as if she were savoring the moment.

His cock hardened to the point of pain. "It's not my best. But thank you."

She opened her eyes and replaced her fork with a spoon. She slid it into the center of the raspberry frosted cupcake, scooped, and lifted it to his lips. "Taste."

The passionate order from her turned him on even more than he was already. He parted his lips and allowed her to feed him a bite of a coffee-drenched sponge cake with raspberry purée and whipped cream frosting. His favorites combined into an explosion of ecstasy in his mouth. She got him in a way no one else would or had ever gotten him.

He licked his lips. She was so close. So beautiful. So loving and nurturing. So sexy as a business owner following her passion and God-given talents. He leaned in and almost kissed her on the lips, but shifted slightly at the last moment, his mouth landing at the corner of hers instead. From anywhere except right above them, it would look as though he had kissed her cheek. A full-on lip-lock was against the rules, but a kiss on the cheek with a small portion of lip fell within regulations. "I love it. My favorite flavors—coffee, raspberry, sugar, and *you*."

She leaned against his side. "Want to come and help me bake this weekend? I need some talented and free labor."

"I suppose it's going to be early mornings?" *I will come and do anything to help you.*

"Yes. But we close early too. Will you?"

"Yeah," he said. "You know I will. But you're

going to have to make me a triple espresso when I arrive."

She snuggled against him, rubbing her soft cheek against his. Her hand slid up his thigh. "I will be happy to hook you up with your caffeine fix."

He covered her hand at his thigh. "You go any higher and I will have trouble controlling myself."

She turned her head and curled her arms around his neck. "I see you and you baked for me. You surprised me. You opened up a world of..." Her tongue peeked between her lips. "I don't know what to do with myself."

You want to make love. You want sex. You want me. "Baby, I want to make a mess in the kitchen with you. Spread raspberry and whipped cream frosting all over you and lick it off." He told himself not to, but he rubbed his cheek against hers and whispered in her ear, "I want you to wear that pink apron and nothing else. I want to come up behind you and bend you over that counter and fuck you. Kitten, I love you. I love you so much."

She shifted and her lips pressed against his ear. "I want that. So badly. Right now. I'm dying." Hot puffs of air whispered into his ear and sent a shock wave of emotion through him. She nibbled on his ear. "I need to be fucked, Jacob. I'm a hot mess. You look so good. So good, and you baked for me."

"I would have baked for you years ago, if I had any clue that was the way to your heart," he mumbled.

She laved over the shell of his ear with her tongue. "I want you to lick my pussy. Make me come. I want to feel you inside me. I need it." Her hand pushed up. "I need to feel your cock. Hard. Needy. Wanting me."

He turned his torso, let go of her hand and cupped her cheeks. "We can't. I'm not going to ruin your life and career. I've done enough damage. I have an idea about how to make you feel better. Hold on. I know there is someone else. I know it's going to be hard and you may even…" *Be honest with her.* "It's easier for me to be faithful. I'm a little older. I've played. I've done things I shouldn't have. I know you're the one for me. I know you're worth waiting for. If you falter, I will be here waiting for you. That's not permission, but, my sweet Sophia, love of my life, I understand the game we're in. A game I had no idea I was involved in until the night had ended. If you find yourself in a place where you feel like you'll regret not knowing what it feels like to be loved by someone else…"

He inhaled and let the words fall and the repercussion of those words be dealt with another day. "When this game is over and all is said and done, I don't want you to have regrets from thoughts of what could have been or what would have been. I have faith in what we have, in who you are, in our future."

He kissed her forehead and then gazed into her blue eyes. "We're going to be together in the end. I am who I am, Sophia. I will screw up. I will make you crazy, but I'll also always be here. I'm not going anywhere. I've always been here." He placed one hand over her heart and the other over his. "You've always been here. In seven weeks, my hands won't be tied, and I will come full-force for you. Nothing and no one will stop me from reclaiming you."

She closed her eyes and held both her hands over his at her chest. "I have never had feelings for anyone but you, until…" She exhaled and looked directly into his eyes. "Seven weeks is a long time."

"I know," he whispered. "I know you'll kiss him. I know you might do more now that the door to those feelings and desires has been opened. I get it, but I'll stop here for a cupcake, find an excuse to have you visit me at work or at home. There are ways around the boundaries we're confined in." *I'm going to figure out a way to take care of you and win. Hudson Fox might be competing for your love, but he's no me.*

She nodded. "You're going to help me Saturday and Sunday, right?"

"I'll double check to make sure helping at the bakery is allowed. As long as it is, I'll be your part-time, free weekend labor." His phone buzzed. "Sorry, I have to take this." He reached into his jacket pocket and read a work text from his executive assistant.

Kellen is out on bail. He has a high-profile attorney. In the underground network, rumor has it that he's done this before, and done worse. I've contracted off-duty police officers to guard Sophia at the bakery. Should I call Sophia so she will let the officers sit in the shop? Remind her that she can refuse Kellen's business and we'll get a restraining order filed. Kellen moved from New York to Pennsylvania to Utah and now he's here. I've got Manny digging. There are two local women missing. I'm worried. Manny said from his initial inquiry, a string of girls have gone missing in the places he's lived around the time he lived there. This isn't an isolated incident, and he's probably pissed Sophia got away.

His hands trembled. He looked around the shop. "Stay here. Do not move." He strode to the only other man in the bakery – Mr. Fox. "I need to speak with you immediately."

Mr. Fox tipped his hat and frowned. "I'm not going to tell my son to stop going after what he wants."

"This isn't about your son. This is about Sophia. Please, I need to talk with you privately." He turned around and hoped to God the man followed him to the front window, away from the customers.

The shuffle and clomp of cowboy boots behind him eased a smidgeon of the fear for Sophia's safety flowing through his veins. Jacob stopped near the window. Mr. Fox joined him.

"My assistant just notified me that the man who murdered Sophia's dog and broke into her apartment is out of jail on bail. Two off-duty police officers are on their way here to guard her while she's here. I'm going to have them come to you. Whatever they need or want, I will pay for. They'll be here waiting for her in the morning and will take shifts until she leaves. I'd prefer they stay inside the bakery. I'd like to talk to Hudson about the situation. I'm about to tell Sophia, but I wanted you to know."

He tapped the screen to his phone and found the text with Kellen's face. "This is the guy. If you see him here, or outside, call the police, and if the officers inside aren't on their way to take care of him, do whatever is necessary to keep him away from Sophia." He opened the contact info and had Mr. Fox enter both his and Hudson's numbers. "I'll be keeping tabs on my girl, and helping her on weekends, but I need to make sure she is *never* alone. Not until this guy is in prison or moved far, far away."

"He won't get anywhere near Sophia. We take care of our own and Sophia is one of us." Mr. Fox patted Jacob on the back like Jacob's father used to do when he was proud of him. "We'll get this guy. And we'll get those officers and their wives hooked on Sophia's goodies. This is serious, but it will be great for business."

"Yeah, but I'm not worried about her business. I'm only worried about her." Jacob walked back to Sophia and sat down.

"Do not strong-arm Mr. Fox. He's supporting his son. Hudson is not a baker. He nearly burned down the first kitchen we built. He can decorate a cupcake in a pinch, but I do not allow him near the oven." She shook her head and huffed and puffed as a bright red spread up her neck and face. "Why do you do that? Just when I'm having those gooey, chocolatey-love feelings for you, you go and play 'my cock is bigger than yours' with a person I care about."

"Kellen made bail. Two police officers will be inside the bakery whenever you're here. If you're going to be here at two in the morning, text me and I'll make sure they are here with you." He stood up and grabbed his wallet from his back pocket. He fished out his personal credit card.

"Use this for all their expenses." He handed it to her as her head dropped an inch forward and her mouth gaped. "They will need to eat and drink, and I am paying for it. I don't want to hear any shit about how strong you are or how you can take care of yourself. I know all that, but we don't know much about that asshole other than *his dick is three inches long*."

Her hands trembled and the red drained from her face, leaving her skin ghost pale.

She was scared. Really scared.

"If he comes anywhere near me, I'm going to… I'm going to…" Her gaze darted from him to the front of the bakery to the counter and back at him.

The normally badass Sophia began to hyperventilate as all her cockiness vanished. Her head dipped down, and defeat seemed to settle into her bones. "He's rich. Really rich. Old money rich. He talked about the shipping industry or diamond mines. He'll buy his way out of this." She made a strangled noise beneath a painful whimper. "What if he comes after you? After the other guys I used to work with? After Mistress Bark? What if—"

Jacob pulled her into his arms and held her. "Don't let him get in your head. Don't let him take your power. Don't worry about me. He wouldn't come after me." He kissed the top of her head. "Just keep your eyes and ears open like normal. If something feels off, trust your instincts and get help. I will do anything to protect you. Absolutely anything."

She trembled, but in true Sophia fashion, she pulled herself together and stepped out of his embrace. "Sorry. Minor meltdown. It's over.

Kellen will be the one needing to make a call. After what he did to me, he'll be lucky if I don't skin h-him." Her voice cracked and her lids fluttered as tears filled her eyes.

"That's my girl. That fucker isn't going to win. Who's going to win?" Jacob tried to hype her up, to get some confidence pumping through her veins again.

"I'm going to win."

"Who's gonna win?" he nodded.

"I'm gonna win," she said louder.

"That's right, baby. Get to baking and fuck the rest of the world. You're the winner. You. Are. The. Winner." He bounced on his heels like he did in his weekly management meetings as he repeated the 'winner' chant once more.

She inhaled and nodded. The woman who he relied on to take care of not only him, but also the people she worked with and managed, found her swagger. "I got this."

"Yes, you do, baby. This ain't nothing you can't handle." *Kellen is not getting within five hundred feet of you or your bakery.*

"I've got to get back to work. Will you take care of this?" She glanced down at the uneaten sandwich and crudité.

"I will, and I'll pick you up for dinner." *I'll call Zane and see if he'll bend the rules about a house visit.* "Text me when you're closing up."

"I'm done at six-thirty. We close at six and with Hudson's parents helping, cleaning up won't take long." She stepped forward and hugged him. "Thank you for lunch. I'm sorry about not eating."

"Shh," he cooed. "No worries. No apologies.

Happy thoughts. I'll be here at six to help with closing. I'm going to need to know what I'm getting into when I show up this weekend." He squeezed her tighter and slid his hand down over her ass. *I want to rub all over you. Get dirty and then clean you up only to get naughty and sticky all over again.*

"I'm going to work you hard this weekend," she whispered.

I'm going to work you out of your clothes tonight. "I sure do hope so."

She snuggled her face against his neck, and he felt her lips press against his flesh.

"Thank you for cleaning up lunch," she said. She pushed back and twirled around. There was a sexy sway to her hips as she walked away. She glanced his way and mouthed *I love you.*

Those three words lowered his stress about her living arrangements with Hudson but intensified his need to protect her from a real threat to her life. He had to do something more. It was time to call in a few favors he'd been holding onto for an emergency. And he needed to find the right puppy for her. Hudson's dog was cute, but she liked Terrier mixes like Rufus and Boxer breeds like Mistress Bark.

As he exited, he recognized the two off-duty police officers approaching the shop. He stopped and chatted briefly with them outside the entrance.

With everyone understanding their role, he felt confident Sophia would be safe while she worked. He strode to his car and began planning seven weeks' worth of activities with Sophia. Stopping her from falling into bed with Hudson wouldn't be easy, but if he played his cards right, he just might be able to manage it.

CHAPTER NINE

———◆———

SOPHIA

STARING AT THE DOOR DIDN'T make Jacob magically appear. Six turned to six-thirty which turned to seven and then eight.

"Send him a text to call when he's done with whatever he's doing," Hudson said. "Or I can take you out tonight."

She gazed up at Hudson and then at the two officers holding their coffees and cupcakes. "Yeah, I'll do that. Dinner would be great. Thanks." She lifted her purse from the hook where her apron hung. *Where are you, Jacob? Why didn't you cancel or call or text me more than an "I'll be late" message?*

The day had been busy and uneventful. With the security of having armed men in the shop who were seemingly thrilled to be there, she put aside her fears of the unknown with Kellen and got lost in the joy of baking and selling happiness and comfort in the form of the best desserts in town.

"I'm going home," she said to the officers. "Thanks for being here. Enjoy the goodies."

One of the men lifted his cupcake. "I have a feeling you're not going to need us once word of your sweets makes it to the precinct. The place is going to be packed with men and women in blue." He strode outside and held the door for his fellow officer.

Hudson locked the front door and walked her out the back. "Text him that you're leaving for the night. He'll worry, and there is nothing to worry about."

She nodded and obeyed his soft order. "I'm not really hungry, and tomorrow is going to be an early morning."

He helped her into his truck and climbed into the driver's seat. "You okay?"

No. "Yeah. I guess I need to look for a place to live. I can't stay with you forever." *I'm sleeping in your bed. Every night I give in a little more to your touch. I reveal more of me, of my struggles, of my hopes and dreams. You share more of yourself. I'm falling in love with you.*

"One thing at a time, sweetheart. You're not moving out while there is uncertainty to the whereabouts of Mr. Pruitt. He could be gone, or he could be lurking in the shadows somewhere nearby or searching for another target. I'm not going to hold you hostage, but I think you're intelligent enough to stay put on my protected property until any threat to your wellbeing is gone." He kept both his hands on the wheel and his voice steady, but the gravity of the situation seemed to weigh on him as much as it did her.

"I don't want to overstay my welcome." *Or do something I may or may not regret.* She checked her phone. *Jacob.*

Sorry. My phone died. My charger broke. An emergency came up as soon as I got in my car to get you. I'm so fucking furious I'm about to break something. Don't fuck Hudson. Damn it. Don't do it. Don't do it because of tonight. You know me. I don't skip out on a plan. I don't have you, so my work life is a series of one fuck up after another. Shit. Got to go.

"Jacob's phone died. Dinner is officially cancelled." *Don't tell him this stuff.* "I'm going to take a shower and head to bed."

Hudson parted his lips as if he were about to say something but instead closed his mouth and remained silent the rest of the drive home.

He parked the truck behind three minivans with wraps of her logo and desserts. "Pick the one you like the most. I hired a morning delivery guy to work for the next few weeks."

"But we didn't discuss—"

He faced her. "It's not something we had to discuss. Offering delivery will pay for itself, and the vans will help market our bakery. Besides, the vans were a gift from my parents which were supposed to arrive before we opened, but we opened a little early. So, it didn't cost either of us anything."

"Why did they buy three? I don't understand why they'd do this."

"They did it because they can, and my mother is thrilled about this business. She wants to be a franchisee at some point. She's got her sister looking for the perfect location." He rolled his eyes. "I love my momma, but she wants to bring your cupcakes to the world. I want to keep it here where we have quality control…" He continued on about his dreams for the bakery which aligned with hers.

They saw eye to eye on the business and most everything else in their lives. Their chance meeting at the grocery store had changed her life. Six months later, they'd hashed out a business plan and a partnership had been born.

"I'm so glad you're in my life," she blurted out. "I couldn't have gotten through the last few days without you." *Why aren't you married? You shouldn't be single.*

"Little lady, I'm the thankful one here. You light up my world whenever you're around." He climbed out of the truck and walked over to her side.

Already accustomed to his gentlemanly ways, she waited for him to open her door.

"I know you don't have much of an appetite, but I made a pot roast in the slow cooker. My parents are on their way to Las Vegas for the evening, but they promised to meet us at the bakery in the morning." He held out his hand. "It would do me some good to talk about our day over dinner. I won't force you to eat, but you need to eat in case you're…" He glanced at her belly and clammed up.

She took his hand and stepped down. *She hadn't thought about the baby she might be carrying, but he remembered her confession. He cared.* "Okay. Dinner would be smart."

"That's my girl." He scooped her up and carried her into the house. "If you're pregnant, do you want a boy or a girl?"

"I don't care. I want a healthy baby, which means I need to eat dinner with you." The scent of roasting meat and vegetables had her salivating and her stomach growling.

"This might be hard to believe, but I can cook the hell out of a crockpot."

She laughed and wrapped her arms around his neck. "I'll be the judge of that."

A low chuckle vibrated in his chest. "I bought you something."

"That new rose muffin pan I wanted?"

"That's arriving at the bakery later this week, but this isn't a business expense."

He placed her on the island counter near the sink and the large slow cooker.

She swung her legs out and in against the base cabinets like a little kid. Something about Hudson made her feel excited, like everything in her life was new and fresh and wonderful. "What, then? Pink oven mitts?"

"Those would be a business expense. No." He grabbed dishes and utensils and brought everything over as he readied the island bar for dinner.

"Tell me what you bought." She couldn't think of a thing that she needed besides underwear, and he wouldn't be buying her lingerie. They might have gotten too close a few times, but he hadn't stepped over the line since the truck incident with his parents.

"I'm rethinking the purchase. I figured you'd have guessed by now. Maybe you don't want it." He ladled the stew into the bowls and placed them on the counter. "How much inventory did you have leftover?"

"Four dozen cookies. The cashew cookies didn't sell at all. I've taken them off the menu. I need to reduce the amount of lemon cookies and increase the chocolate chip ones. The big sellers are the cupcake of the day and the trio of croissants." She slid from the cabinet and walked around the island to the chair next to his at the bar.

"My mom said the raspberry mocha torte should be on the regular menu." He filled cups with ice water and joined her.

"I'll consider it. It's too soon to add to the basic menu." She lifted a spoonful of carrots and beef to her mouth. *Smells good, but he can't bake to save his life. Please don't let this be awful.*

She glanced at the door to the half bath in the hall and tried to calculate the time it would take for her to get there, if the potential for an instant puking became all too real.

"You look afraid to try it. I promise it's good."

"No. Not at all," she replied.

"Then try it," he said. "You won't be disappointed."

I hope I'm not disappointed. I do not want to puke right now. "You only live once," she mumbled, and committed to the tasting. Savory, sweet, sour, and salty goodness met her taste buds. "This is delicious."

"Told you it was good." He leaned over and kissed her cheek. "Thanks for the compliment. Tomorrow, I'm making Texas chili. You haven't lived until you've eaten my chili. I'm making that in the slow cooker, too."

"I'm down for that." She crossed her legs as heat built up between them. *I need to calm down and not think what the thought of him cooking does to me. The way to my heart is through my stomach.*

He unbuttoned his suit jacket and placed his cowboy hat on the counter. "Excuse me. I seem to have forgotten my manners."

"How was your day?" They always talked about her day. Her life. Her dreams. Her problems. She needed to focus on him for a change. "What did you do?"

He inhaled and leaned back in the bar chair. The long exhale that escaped from him seemed to say more than he had intended. "I went to a funeral. One of my employee's daughters passed away unexpectedly. Heart issue that went undiagnosed. The girl had soccer scouts salivating over her last week and now..." He trailed off with a sigh. "It was a challenging day."

I'm a selfish jerk. "I'm so sorry. Is there anything I can do?"

"You can help by eating," he said.

She picked up her spoon and made a conscious effort to eat more quickly than usual.

"Thanks." He looked down at his half-empty bowl.

"How are her parents?" she asked.

"They're amazing. I don't know how they're keeping it together. They have a faith that is unshakeable." He picked up his spoon and began eating again. "I can't stop thinking about how young she was and how random it all seemed. She was healthy, beautiful, smart, and kind." He seemed to shovel the stew into his mouth to stop the downward spiral of sadness over a girl's life that was cut short.

"Are you okay?" She nudged him with her elbow. "Need time alone? I can call Angie and take Haus off your hands for the night." *Zane will be furious if I bring over the puppy. I can't stay there. I could go to—*

"No. Haus is with my parents in Vegas. I'm sure he's having a grand time. I'm okay. I thought about how quickly things change. I could have lost you last week without ever knowing you had been in danger. Life is short and sometimes you have to—"

Her phone rang.

She held up her hand. "Hold that thought. This might be another cupcake order." She grabbed her purse on the counter and dug through it.

"Need this?" Hudson held her phone.

"Yes." She skimmed her fingers over the side of his hand as she took it from him. *You are so easy to be with. No drama. No rollercoaster rides with you.*

The phone rang in her hand, prompting a quick swipe. "Sophia's Sweets. This is Sophia."

"It's Blake. Jacob is in the hospital. He's fine. He's got a broken—"

"What?" she said louder than she meant to. "What happened?"

"There was a car accident…" Blake continued talking but all she heard was *accident, car, totaled.*

"I'll be right there," she said. "Does he have a room?"

"He's in surgery," Blake said.

"Oh, God, no." She couldn't breathe. *He doesn't*

have any family. He has me. He only has me, and I was about to give up on him. "I'll text you when I get there." She slid from her bar chair. "I have to go." She gazed up at Hudson. "I'm sorry. It's Jacob. He's hurt. I'm not supposed to see him, but I have to go. I can't not go. I—"

Hudson took her hand and moved with purpose like a man used to taking control of bad situations. "I'll get you there. This is all my doing, Sophia. It's my decision to take you. Don't worry about anything. I promise this will not blow back on you for any reason whatsoever."

As if he knew about her contract with Pussy Pleasures, he soothed her fears as he guided her into his truck. He made her believe nothing could touch her or her business. That her world wasn't crashing down around her again.

"I'm going to lose everything, Hudson," she mumbled. *Please, Lord, watch over Jacob and keep him alive. I love him. Don't take him away from me, too.*

"You're not losing anyone or anything. I'm going to make sure you receive your heart's desires. All of them," Hudson said.

She took a leap of faith and believed him.

CHAPTER TEN

———

JACOB

LAYING ON A HOSPITAL BED in the middle of the VIP section of the hospital hallway was not Jacob's idea of a good time. He was still a little groggy from surgery. Being hooked up to an IV and getting ready to be connected to monitoring equipment had not been in his plans for the evening, but neither had surgery.

The nurse rolled him into the huge VIP suite. "You've got visitors, Mr. Bell."

He knew that. Blake was there. Had been there. Would continue to be there until Jacob was chauffeured home. Now that he had a cast on his arm and was stable, he was ready to leave.

Unfortunately, the doctor wanted to have every test known to man run and checked before Blake could take him home. Being on the board of directors at the hospital had its privileges and its disadvantages. All he wanted to do was to figure out a way to see Sophia.

"Just get the release paperwork and Blake Greystoke will sign them so I can finally go home." *This is cautious taken to a whole other level.* He pushed up in the bed and groaned. "Shit. Can you get those extra pain meds?"

"Once I get you—"

"Jacob," Sophia's voice cut off the nurse.

"Sophia?" He jerked up into a seated position. "Why are you here?" *You're here. Damn. You're here with him.*

She rushed over with her gorgeous raven hair flowing over her shoulders and those sweet blue eyes filled with tears and worry. She grabbed the bed rail and insisted she help the nurse position the bed near the monitors. The nurse had no recourse, not with his Sophia on task.

Once the bed was in place, Sophia climbed up and wrapped her arms around his neck. "I love you. I was so scared."

He curled his right arm around her. The pain of the surgery vanished at the joy of holding her. "I love you. I'm sorry you were scared. I'm fine. A couple screws in my arm, and they made me good as new." *I think that's all they did.*

"I'm going to lose everything by being here, but—"

"You love me," he whispered. "Marry me, Sophia. Please, marry me."

"Are you drugged up?" she whispered.

"Yeah, but I'm thinking clearly, baby. Marry me and let's take on this life together."

She leaned back and gazed into his eyes.

You are so beautiful, my lovely wife. "How can I convince you to marry me again? I will do anything."

"Get in a car accident?" she asked. A heavy

sigh full of disappointment seemed to tug her lips down into a frown.

He'd caused her to doubt his intentions, and he had to make all that up to her. He'd spend the rest of his life erasing all her doubts.

"Anything but that." *Do you think I did this on purpose?*

Her cheek twitched, and a slight smile appeared and then vanished from her lips. "Good to hear. I know how much you loved that car."

"I love you more." *More than anything in the world. I would choose you over all the money and cars in the world.*

Hudson walked over. "Blake had to leave. Something about Lis needing a special kind of ice cream."

"Oh. Doesn't surprise me." *Leave me here while I can't fight for Sophia. Blake, you're such an asshole, and I'm going to tell you so as soon as I see you.*

"Zane will be here in a few minutes," Hudson said. "The police picked up Kellen after he tried to flee the scene of the accident. He hit you on purpose. They also found the two missing college girls. They were dead in his trunk. There is no getting out of that."

"He's the one who hit me?" *He had a corpse in the trunk? No fucking way.*

"Yeah. Several of the surveillance cameras recorded the crash. Lots of witnesses. Dude tried to run." Hudson rolled his eyes. "He ran into a brick wall and knocked himself out."

"No shit?"

"Seriously. He did." Hudson turned his head

toward the door, prompting Jacob to look the same way.

"There's my man," Zane said. "Buddy, it's good to see you looking so…" Zane's face contorted. "You look like you were on the wrong side of a cage match."

"Thanks, Zane. How are all of Angie's rescue puppies treating your beautifully manicured yard?" Jacob asked. *I may not be on my A-game, but don't screw with me.*

Zane clenched his jaw tight. "You're about to find out, asshole. Sophia is homeless, Lis hates you, and Hudson offered to put you up, but I told him you're better off hanging with me and Angie. Mistress Bark is already at my house and attempted to teach those digging fuckers to stop, but she failed. Instead of being a good girl, she gave in to their muses and showed them how to dig a huge fucking trench down the left side of my newly sodded lawn. You're paying to fix that."

"Dogs are pack animals," Hudson interjected in what seemed like defense of Jacob's dog, Mistress Bark. "Now they have a leader to follow," Hudson said. "I'm not having any problems with my puppy, uh, Sophia's pup. He's sleeping through the night and follows me around at work. Won't be long before he's stationed for guard duty at the bakery."

"What's his name?" Jacob asked. He gazed at Sophia, but her focus remained on Hudson.

"We haven't really named him," Hudson said. "The guys call him Haus. I use hand signals and snap my fingers to call him. Sophia hasn't been able to spend much time with him."

"You and Blake can train any animal. I hate you two," Zane mumbled. He dropped a green and red reusable grocery bag on the end of the bed near Jacob's feet. "Sophia, you need to leave. Jacob is changing, not that you haven't seen a penis before, but Jacob's might frighten you by how small it is."

Hudson outright belly-laughed. "Come on, sugar. Zane is going to help Tiny get his clothes on."

"I do not have a small cock," Jacob said.

Sophia faced him and gently traced the bruises on his cheek. She kissed above the butterfly stitches on his forehead and whispered, "I know. Believe me, I know." She carefully caressed along his neck and shoulder before taking Hudson's offered hand and climbing off the bed. "I'm sure I'll see you soon."

Her shoulders slouched and her head hung low.

"Head up," Jacob said. "Shoulders back."

In less than a millisecond, she obeyed him and walked like a woman of substance out of the room.

As soon as the door closed, Zane moved to the side of the bed. "She doesn't believe you love her. That's on you. You and Angie joining forces over a puppy for Sophia—well, that is not acceptable. I have ten puppies at my house. Right. Now. Waiting for your ass to pick one for Kitten 43." He glared at Jacob and lowered his voice even more. "I'm about to tell the other lover no condoms required. If she ends up pregnant, you two will force a paternity test. Ratings will skyrocket. I'll lose my bet with Blake over this, but it would be worth it. I put my money on you. Blake thinks Hudson is going to be the victor. Lis and Angie are furious with both of us."

"This is your fault, not mine," Jacob said. "Sophia needs me. Hudson has her so busy she can't grieve. You added the puppy into this mix. It's too soon for a puppy. She got one and hasn't claimed it or it would be with her all the time. That dog ain't going home with her when she leaves his house, and she *will* leave his house permanently for mine." He grabbed the bed rail and pulled himself up. He held in a grunt and a scream as pain shot through his left side and arm.

Zane's piercing blue eyes might intimidate other men, but not Jacob.

"Let me tell you something," Jacob said. "You might use my passionate nature against me, but I *can* control myself. Hudson is not fucking my wife. And she is my wife, isn't she?"

Zane looked away.

"You sonofabitch," Jacob grumbled. "She is, and she thinks she's not. She wouldn't go anywhere near Hudson if she thought for a millisecond our marriage was real. It is real. It is filed already, and you're playing her against me. Shame on you, Zane. You're going to push her too far. If she ends up having a moment of weakness…" *I'm going to kill you.* "Does Hudson know she's really married to me?"

"Get dressed," Zane said.

"He doesn't." *I've got to get the hell out of here and tell them the truth.* "You're playing a game that is going to hurt people. Hurt them for years to come." He took the blue pajama pants out of the bag and grunted as he moved every which way in order to get dressed by himself.

"All three of you signed up for the show. No one forced any of you into it." Zane strode to the window.

"No. But the show has lied to them and to me. Sophia and Hudson will end up committing adultery and that is on you." *I'm going to stop them.*

"I don't think they will," Zane said. "She loves you."

"She loves him too," Jacob said. "Not like she loves me, but she loves him. He's a great, upstanding guy. He doesn't deserve to be played like this. He's ethical and this will devastate him." *I can't believe I'm saying this about him.*

"If she loves you, she won't want to even try," Zane mumbled.

"Don't make this about you and Angie," Jacob's voice rose. "You fucked with Angie so much that she left and went to someone else she loved. She loved you more, but *you* pushed her past her limit. You're not doing the same to my Sophia. Angie forgave you for pushing her away and you forgave her. She loves you with her heart and soul and everything else that lives and breathes within her. She gets you. Don't push my Sophia. She's been through hell. Losing her parents last year, and now losing Rufus, is too much. She would have been dead if she weren't an overachieving businesswoman. Don't punish her, or me."

"She seems to have moved on quickly enough," Zane retorted.

"Zane Winslow," Jacob said. "She hasn't moved on. You don't move on from what she's been through. You learn how to live with it, and she hasn't done that yet. The bakery is a distraction. Kellen in jail is a distraction. Hudson is a distraction. I'm not a distraction. I'm a reminder of what she lost. She thinks she lost me. That is on you, and you're going to fix it."

Zane glanced at him. "I'm not fixing anything."

Jacob pressed the button for the nurse. He couldn't get a shirt on, not with the cast. Not without cutting off a sleeve.

An older nurse with sparkles of gray throughout her dark hair walked in carrying a tray with a folder and medicine on it. "Your ears must have been burning. I was just talking about you." She placed the silver tray on the bed. "I see Mr. Winslow will be taking you home."

"Yes," Jacob said. "Zane, I need to make a quick call with your phone."

Zane's eyes seemed to burn with anger as he joined the nurse next to the bed. He handed over his cellphone. "Make it quick."

The nurse went through the doctor's instructions and next appointments, along with the rest of patient release protocol.

Jacob hung onto Zane's phone until the nurse left to get a wheelchair so he could leave.

He scrolled though Zane's contacts for Hudson's number. In a few taps, Hudson answered the phone.

"This is Jacob. Could you please come get me at the hospital and take me home? I'm not in any shape to drive, and they won't let me call a service to take me home."

"Zane isn't taking you home?"

"Zane and I are…" *I want to fuck Zane over so*

damn bad. But I can't. I won't. "We're in a minor ethical argument and can't seem to come to an agreement on the right thing to do."

"That's no good."

"No. It's not." *How do I tell you about Zane's games without saying anything about Pussy Pleasures and getting slapped with another fine?* "I need to tell you something. It's complicated, but Sophia and I got married a few days ago. Only, we got into a fight and then got a call that there was a problem with the license and our marriage was basically void. Only, we are married. There wasn't a mistake with *our* license in the State of Nevada, and our marriage is recognized as valid. She's angry with me, and I don't blame her. I know you two are close and seem to be getting closer by the minute. I don't want her to do something that she will regret because she was given false information."

"Is this a stunt to stop Sophia from leaving you for good?" Hudson asked.

"No. This is one hundred percent true. Sophia should be getting a call soon, verifying it. I'm sorry you're caught up in the middle of our drama. You're a good guy, Hudson, and I hope that we can be friends. Sophia made a solid decision by partnering with you in her bakery."

"I'm turning the car around. You better be telling me the truth. I want verification by the time I arrive at the hospital."

Jacob tilted his head to get a better glimpse of Zane's reaction. A sharp pain hammered against his skull and spine at the movement, but this game had to end today. The veins in Zane's neck bulged.

The guy he'd known since middle school seemed unusually upset. Something was up, and it had nothing to do with his matchmaking project.

"I'll get you verification," Jacob said. "A photo of the license is being sent to Zane's phone since mine is broken."

"Okay," Hudson said. "See you soon." He ended the call before Jacob could reply.

"I need a photo of the marriage license. Now." He handed the phone over to Zane. "You can do that, can't you?"

"Yes." Zane sat down on the light-blue pleather chair next to the bed. His fingers flew across the screen at lightning speed. "You always win, Jacob."

"What has got you so worked up you're screwing with your friends' lives? What you did to Lis was crazy. What you're doing with me and Sophia is not like you. Talk to me." *Are you trying to punish me or yourself?*

Zane closed his eyes. "Angie has cancer. She's seven months pregnant. They can't do anything. She's trying to make it long enough to give the baby a fighting chance. Her weight loss and all the symptoms seemed like they were extreme side effects of pregnancy. They didn't check for cancer for a long time. We went to specialists all over the world, and last week a nutritionist in an herbalist's office made an offhand comment about how her symptoms sounded like pancreatic cancer." He stood up. "That nutritionist set us on a different path. Angie is dying, and the baby isn't doing well."

"Oh, my God." *No. Not that.* "Can they treat her

as soon as the baby comes?"

"They don't expect her to make it that long. I don't want to talk about it anymore. I'll call Hudson so he doesn't leave Sophia alone." He walked toward the door to leave. "I'm sorry. I'm fucking sorry, but I—"

"Buddy?" Jacob said.

Zane glanced over his shoulder. Tears stained his eyes. "Yeah?"

"Give me your phone. I'll text Hudson. I'm going home with you just like I did in middle school when the news came in about your mom. We'll figure this out together. Pull the car around front and wait for me." The marriage license for Sophia would have to wait.

"You'd come home with me?"

"Yeah, man. I may be banged up and a pain in your ass, but you need me. Has Angie told anyone?" *You're reliving your mother's death. You finally have everything you ever wanted and it's being stripped away from you.*

"No. She brought home puppies. She's on a massive rescuing mission. I want her to slow down more, but she's out trying to rescue every dog in Nevada in the time she has left." He inhaled. "I just want her to live. I can't do life without her. Not now that I know what living truly feels like."

"You've got me and Blake and Lis and Sophia. Your dad is a phone call away. We'll help you through this."

Zane nodded as he turned toward the door. "I'm sorry. I don't know what to do with myself. Angie is in so much pain, but she won't take the medicine the doctor prescribed because of the potential side effects to the baby. It won't be long before she doesn't have a choice and has to take something more than herbal medicine to help her through the day."

"How long do they think she's been sick?" *All the times you cancelled last minute because Angie wasn't feeling well...*

As he connected the dots to the last year of their friendship and Angie's weight loss, her stomach issues, her slowing down, exhaustion, and all the recent trips overseas, Jacob's heart ached to ease his best friend's pain. *I don't know what I'd do if I lost Sophia.*

"They suspect she's had it close to two years. But she's been pregnant all but four months out of the last three." He hunched farther and farther over as the silence he'd kept for so long came flowing out in one long release. "Once they began testing, the labs came back positive. Positive. Positive. Positive. Stage 4. Stage 4. Stage 4. Stage 4. We couldn't believe it, so we got more tests. All the results were the same. All the same ending. One or both of them will die." He opened the door. "I texted Hudson. He'll tell Sophia in the morning. I'll pull the car around and meet you in front."

"Zane, is there a chance for a miracle?"

"It's spread to her lungs and bones. The doctors have that look in their eyes. You know the one. The one my dad gave me when he talked about my mom." Zane strode out of the room.

The problems Jacob faced with Sophia didn't seem insurmountable anymore. Sophia was safe. Once a copy of the marriage license was forwarded to Hudson, the man wouldn't pursue

Sophia anymore. All Jacob had to do was show Sophia how much he loved her. With the news Zane shared about Angie, Jacob realized life was too short and every day allowed him a chance to show his love to his wife and friends. Angie was one of the best people he'd ever met, and she and Zane had a life most people dreamed of having—a life Jacob would have with Sophia. Only, now his buddy's perfect life wasn't perfect anymore. The love Zane never thought he'd find was being tragically stripped from him.

A pretty blond-haired nurse wearing dark green scrubs rolled a wheelchair into the room. "Ready to go home, Mr. Bell?"

"Yes, thank you," Jacob said.

She helped him into the chair. "Is Mr. Winslow okay to drive you home?" She squatted in front of him, flipped the foot rests down, and guided his feet onto them. "He seemed upset when he got into the elevator."

As she gazed up at him, deep pools of worry seemed to swirl in her blue eyes. A classic beauty, the young nurse would have stopped him in his tracks years ago, but his thoughts went to Sophia and then to his best friend's wife.

Zane has to be okay. He's got two kids to take care of. They're losing the center of their family. "He's going to be okay to drive me home."

"I wouldn't normally offer this, but since both of you are on the board here, let me—well, my brother—drive both of you home. Mr. Winslow can pick up his car tomorrow."

Maybe it was the pain meds kicking in, but he thought for a moment there was something special about this girl and her offer of a ride sounded like a course of action he had to accept.

"That would be great. I wouldn't have accepted if it were you driving us. I don't care how normal a person may seem to be, you can't—"

"I'm a good judge of character. It's the only real natural skill I have. The rest I work hard to master." She stood up. "I'm not letting Mr. Winslow get behind the wheel for an extended period of time. And I'm definitely not releasing you without handing you off to a person who is thinking clearly." She stared down at him. Her strength of character and ethical standards blew him away. "So, either you tell him, or I will."

I can't believe you're playing hardball with two people who could get you fired with a quick text.

"Your silence speaks loud and clear." She walked around him and wheeled him out of the room. She grabbed her purse at the nurses' station, waved and said her farewells, and rolled him down a hall, into an elevator, and out to the patient pick-up area.

Zane stood beside Angie's black minivan with the sliding door opened.

A champagne-colored SUV pulled up behind Zane's car. A man with short blond hair and blue eyes wearing makeup and a canary-yellow business suit and white slip-ons stepped out of the driver's seat and leaned up against the car door.

"Madison Claire Morgan, do not do what I think you're about to do," the man said, swirling his hand until it stopped and his finger pointed at her.

Madison ignored her brother but extended her arm and flapped her hand in his direction. "Get back in your car, Andy."

She approached Zane as if nothing out of the ordinary was happening.

"Mr. Winslow," Madison said. "I need you to go and park your car in one of the empty spaces."

"No," Zane said.

The girl snapped her fingers at her brother. "Help Mr. Bell into your car, Andy."

As Madison walked to Zane, Andy sashayed over to Jacob. "You have to be Mr. Bell. Please tell me I'm just driving you somewhere, and you're not coming home with us for the night."

"Driving," Jacob answered, but his gaze stayed on Madison and Zane.

"Don't watch. Madison is a stickler for driver protocol. Our father died in a fatal car crash. Maddie told him not to get behind the wheel that day." Andy leaned over and whispered, "The other driver wanted to die, and our father's 18-wheeler looked like it could do the job. He lived. Our father died. That man she's talking to looks like a guy who is super depressed, not suicidal. Although I could be wrong. Maddie's got the gift, not me."

Jacob put his arm around the kid who didn't look like much, but the hard muscle underneath all that bright yellow was substantial.

"Let me do the work, big guy," Andy said.

Jacob stared at Zane arguing with the headstrong nurse.

"I hope he gives in for a change and comes with us," Jacob said.

"Maddie will get her way. No one can sway her once her mind is made up," Andy said.

"My friend is as stubborn as they come."

"Not like my sister."

"No," Madison shouted. "Get your ass in my brother's SUV. You are not driving. If I have to, I'll drive you home myself."

"You're not—" Zane yelled.

Madison snatched Zane's keys out of his hand and climbed into the minivan. She closed the door and rolled down the window. "Get in the car." She started the engine. "Don't fuck with me, or I'll start crying and you do not want that to happen."

Andy let out a heavy sigh. "He's pushed her button. She only has one that I'm aware of. God help him because He's the only one capable of stopping Maddie when she gets on a roll."

To Jacob's amazement, Zane slammed the sliding door, stomped to the other side of the car, and climbed in the passenger's side.

Andy helped Jacob into the car and then ran around and hopped into the driver's side. "Wherever I need to take you is going to have to wait. I have to follow her first." He started the engine and rolled forward, keeping to the higher end of the speed limits in the parking lot as he followed Maddie.

"We're going to the same place. And, I'll have to thank you and your sister for tonight. Zane shouldn't be driving, and I can't drive." He rattled off Zane's address and closed his eyes. *I should be going to Zane's with my wife. When she finds out about Angie, it's going to devastate her.* "If you were married—"

"I am married," Andy said. "His name is Hector."

"Oh. Perfect. Let's say you messed up. You put

your relationship and his business in jeopardy because you thought you could pay your way out of a game you hadn't expected to be in."

"Sorry goes a long way," Andy said.

"Sorry isn't enough. I broke some rules and now we're both paying for it, but she's got this contract that I think has to do with my actions. What would you do if you were me?"

"Tell her you love her and take yourself out of the equation until you can find a way to terminate both contracts," Andy said.

"But I want to win," Jacob said.

"How much do you love her?" Andy asked.

"More than the world. She's everything to me."

"Love her enough to lose some time with her. The real winning is having her love, isn't it?"

"Yeah, it is."

Madison stopped at the security guard station at the gated entrance to Jacob and Zane's neighborhood. She leaned her head out and looked at them. She reached out and held the security guard's hand for a second, and when she let go, the guard stood a little taller.

She drove forward as the gate opened.

The security guard waved them through.

Andy's casual demeanor changed to formal as they drove farther and farther into the exclusive community. He straightened his spine as they entered through Zane's privacy gate.

"Are you Jacob Bell, Zane Winslow's best friend?" Andy said barely above a whisper.

"Yes, I am."

"Oh." Andy parked the car behind the minivan in the driveway on the side of the house. "It was a pleasure to meet you."

The man who'd treated Jacob like a friend suddenly became a stranger.

"Did I do something to make you uncomfortable?" Jacob asked.

"No, no." Andy got out of the car and then helped Jacob out. "Do you have someone to get your meds?"

"I can get a friend to get them."

"If you run into any trouble, call me. I'm easy to find in a google search," Andy said.

"Zane Winslow." Maddie's voice rose from the silence in a low sexy growl. "If you bitch one more time about those puppies to her, I will personally come over and take you over my knee. Do you hear me?"

"Who the fuck do you think you are?" Zane said in a deep grumble.

"I am the only one who won't put up with your shit. Get inside and hug your kids and wife. Make love to the woman because you don't know how long you two will have that intimacy, if you still do." She punched Zane's arm. "Get some balls and grow the fuck up."

"Oh, shit," Andy groaned. "Please don't get her fired."

"He's not like that," Jacob mumbled.

Maddie walked away but turned her head toward him. "Stop being so fucking selfish."

"Fuck you," Zane shouted.

She spun around. "Fuck you, you whiny piece of shit."

"My wife is dying," Zane screamed.

"My fiancé died from pancreatic cancer. You're

not the only one who has gone through this. You're not the only fucking one who knows what it's like to lose the person you love more than yourself. Suck it up and give her every bit of love you have inside you and know that it may be the only time in your life you will ever be with someone you love the way God intended—with all your heart, mind, body, and soul. Cherish this time with her. Don't piss it away because you got dealt a shitty card. She wouldn't do that to you. Stew on that."

"Come on, Maddie," Andy shouted. "This is not your fight. You got them both home safely."

Maddie turned around, her face red and pained. She ran past Jacob and Andy to the SUV and climbed into the passenger seat.

Zane covered his face with his hands as Jacob and Andy approached.

"I'm sorry, Mr. Winslow," Andy said. "Her loss was recent, and it was one in a string of unfortunate losses." He somehow transitioned Jacob from his arms to Zane's.

"Tell her I'm sorry. I didn't know. I'm sorry," Zane mumbled.

"Don't worry about it. She'll most likely apologize to you when she sees you again," Andy said.

Zane supported Jacob as he shuffled toward the front door. "Take care of her, Andy. I'm sorry."

"Please don't get her fired," Andy said. "She's a great nurse, and she's passionate about helping people."

"I won't," Zane mumbled.

"Please," Andy begged. "Don't get her fired."

"I won't," Zane repeated as he opened the door

to the house. "Go home."

The door closed behind them.

Zane fell apart and began sobbing. "I can't live without her."

"You're going to have to," Jacob said. "You have two toddlers." Jacob had no idea where the strength came from, but he held Zane up.

"She's so sick," Zane sobbed.

"I got you, man," Jacob said. "Tomorrow, we'll talk about how Blake and I can help you run your businesses, so you can focus on the only thing that matters—your family."

The strength that had always carried Jacob through the worst of times would carry his best friend for as long as he needed. Jacob might be bruised and broken, but he could take on another burden. He could take on a thousand burdens to ease his buddy's pain, to support Angie, to protect Sophia, to carry all of them into a future filled with the ups and downs of life.

Holding Zane, Jacob felt a renewed sense of fight. They might not be able to save Angie, but they would make her last months filled with the most important gift any of them could give–love.

CHAPTER ELEVEN

———

SOPHIA

"**S**UGAR," HUDSON WHISPERED IN HER ear. "Are you awake?"

I've been up for hours. "Mmm," she mumbled.

For days, Jacob hadn't called. Zane hadn't called. Angie hadn't called. No marriage license photo. No call from Pussy Pleasures. Another week gone without a word or a return text from any of them. The only people she heard from were the prosecutors of the Kellen Pruitt case. The man might still be in jail, but his high-profile attorney was making a strong case in the court of public opinion. The coverage of Kellen on the nightly news had her crawling into Hudson's bed at night.

He pulled her closer. "I don't know what is going on, but if I were Jacob, I'd have at least taken someone's phone and called you by now. Do you think he and Zane cooked up that whole marriage story?"

She hated that she questioned Jacob's word, but she did. She questioned his word enough to spend another night wrapped up in Hudson's arms imagining a life of raising children in a loving relationship with grandparents ready to dote on them. It would be so easy to step over the line—she was already partially there.

"Neither one of them are liars. They're honest. They might stretch the truth or omit something, but they're good people." *Angie would have called me if she thought the marriage was real. I need to call her. Ask her what she's heard from Jacob and Zane.*

"If we don't hear anything today"—Hudson rolled on top of her and pushed her legs apart—"I'm going to call one of my guys to see what he can find."

She flushed with warmth in places she wasn't sure she should allow him to access. She squeezed her legs together, but his powerful thighs were no match. Instead of telling him no, she curled her legs around his hips and pulled him closer until his cock pressed firmly between her legs.

"Uhn," he mumbled. "Sugar, this isn't something we can undo."

"I've only been with one man. I thought he'd—" She shut her mouth and refused to explain. She loved Jacob. She'd always been able to count on him, but now that they were…*What are we, Jacob? I don't even know.* "I can't promise anything. I don't know if this door we're considering opening would lead to marriage."

"I can," Hudson said. "If we do this, it will be incredible, and we will get hitched." He kissed her lips. "I want marriage and babies, and I want them now."

"I do, too." *But are we supposed to be together?*

Would you do what Jacob does? Would you take me, knowing I liked something I didn't know I liked until you did it?

Hudson rubbed his scruffy cheek against hers. His warm lips caressed the shell of her ear. "I want you so badly, Sophia."

He thrust and her pussy contracted. Hard. Her clit begged for more. *Rip my clothes off. Jacob would. Jacob would have his cock out and fucking me so hard. Why aren't you doing that? Why aren't you taking me? I'm here. In your bed. Are you waiting for more of an invitation?*

Her phone buzzed on the nightstand. Then Angie's ringtone blared.

"I have to answer this," she said.

He inhaled and blew softly into her ear. "Yeah." He exhaled hard. "Okay. Okay." He flopped onto his back, off her.

Rolling away from him, she wished he'd have asked her not to answer. Jacob would have demanded her attention. Demanded her body. They would argue and the temperature and desire would rise between them.

She answered the phone. "Need some cupcakes?"

"It's Jacob. I need you to come to Zane's and get me."

"Call a driver."

"No. I need *you.* Sophia, I have our marriage license and certificate. The man who married us is a pastor. Our license was filed with the state and it is legal. I got a special circumstances waiver to see you for an hour. So much has happened. Please, Sophia. Please come get me."

The desperation in his voice wasn't her Jacob.

He didn't beg. Not like that. She'd have to check with Pussy Pleasures for confirmation that she was allowed to see him, but if she did, then she might get slapped with another fine or lose her partnership in the bakery.

"I'm going to have to check on a few things, but I'll do my best to get there soon." She sat up and began her morning routine as she listened to his instructions. "Hang on."

Dressed and ready to go, she held the phone to her chest. "I've got to go to Zane's for a few minutes. I'll meet you and your mom at the bakery."

"Yes, ma'am." Gorgeous Hudson stood beside the bed with a look that made her want to drop the phone and get naked, but her heart wasn't in it, not like before.

The man who continued to rule her heart needed her and she had to go to him.

"If I miss you at the bakery, I'm taking Haus to work with me. The guys love having him around. If you need any help or if Jacob shows up and you don't want to talk to him, call me. I'll come for you."

"Thanks. I'm sorry I haven't done anything with the puppy. I've just been absorbed with making sure the bakery is successful." She inhaled. *Haus is yours, not mine.* She kissed his cheek. "I'm going to see if Jacob is telling the truth and there is a real marriage license."

"I hope it's all fake," Hudson whispered.

She couldn't say the same. Hudson was a good man who would make a wonderful husband, but he wasn't Jacob.

"Thanks for everything," she whispered. She

reached out and squeezed his hand. "Stay away from the oven."

"I'm just there to help put cupcakes in boxes," he said.

"That's what I wanted to hear." She walked out of the bedroom and through the house to her car.

In the privacy of her car, she turned it on and jumped as the phone transitioned to hands-free. She'd forgotten to hang up her cell. If Jacob had heard her with Hudson, he'd know how close they'd gotten. *Should I call Blake to pick Jacob up?*

"Are you still there, Sophia?" Jacob asked.

"Yeah. I'm here." She drove off of Hudson's property and toward Zane's house. "I only have an hour before I have to be at the bakery."

"You might need to take the day," Jacob said.

She'd had enough. The anxiety surrounding all the manipulations, the breaking of rules, the loss of her dog, and the Kellen Pruitt case proved too much to hold in any longer.

"I'm not taking the day off. I'll bring you home, but then I'm heading to the bakery. No one and nothing is going to stop me from making my life and business a success. I'm translating what that means because you don't seem to understand. It means showing up at work to bake, because I don't have a staff. I *can't* take a day off because my supposed husband wants me to obey his every order. Not happening, Jacob. Not happening. *Ever.*"

She ended the call and hit the accelerator. *I am not wasting any more time. If he doesn't produce a marriage license, I'm done. I'll be Mrs. Hudson*

Fox as soon as my obligation to Pussy Pleasures is over.

The phone rang again.

Against her better judgement, she answered.

"Sophia," Jacob said.

"I'm almost there." Hudson lived on the other side of the secret power quad's exclusive neighborhood. Zane Winslow, Jacob Bell, Blake Greystoke, and Nathaniel Griffin handpicked those allowed to buy property and build in their private billionaire community, and Hudson probably didn't fit into their boys' club. *Ugh. I'm so done with all of this.*

She waved to the security guard and, to her surprise, he opened the gate without having her stop. *You've always made me stop and answer questions like who I was seeing and how long I was staying when I came to visit Jacob or Angie or Lis.* "The security guard let me pass without stopping."

"You're my wife. You can come and go as you please," Jacob said.

"But what about documentation?" *They need paperwork. It took two days before they didn't stop Angie.*

"The paperwork is filed and accepted by the HOA. The guards know you."

"I almost did things with Hudson. I didn't. We didn't."

"Baby, I'm so glad you didn't give in to his charms. I'm so glad you waited, that you had faith in us."

But I didn't. I didn't believe you. I'm not sure I believe you now. Why do I feel like I need to tell you how far things had gone with Hudson?

Confessing seemed like the right thing to do, but her throat constricted and nothing came out. She whipped around the corners, driving too fast, but at that time of morning the neighborhood had very little activity.

"I would have made love to him, if he had tried," she mumbled. *Thank God Hudson hadn't pushed. I would be a mess.* "Does this mean we're moving in together?" *The show hadn't contacted me about any changes.*

The gate to Zane's property lifted and she continued onward and parked in the drive behind Zane's minivan. "What is the minivan doing outside the entrance?"

"Are you here?" Jacob asked.

"Yes," she said. She exited her car and walked toward the front door.

Jacob opened the door and hobbled forward.

She rushed to him. "Lean on me." *You didn't seem this injured at the hospital last week. What happened? What's going on?*

Jacob put his arm over her shoulder and accepted her help. "Lis and Blake have Angie and Zane's kids for the week. We're all going to have to pitch in to help Zane and Angie with the kids."

"What's going on?" *Angie wouldn't go through you to set up babysitting. I do that. She calls me.*

"Blake and Lis and I have spent this week helping Zane and Angie make plans for the kids, the businesses, and their future. I would have called before now, but..." Jacob hesitated and then gritted his teeth as he tried to maneuver into the small interior of her convertible.

With a bit of mumbling and a few curt words by

both of them, she managed to get him into the car.

They can't be divorcing. Angie would have told me. The dogs aren't that big of an issue. Zane might be angry, but not enough to consider leaving her.

She slipped into the driver's seat and drove toward Jacob's property in the part of the neighborhood that was left undeveloped. Jacob owned that quarter of the development. He had plans to sell a parcel of the land if the right person came along and asked—at least, that was what he'd told her years ago.

"I know you have a bakery to run," Jacob said. "But I have to tell you something and it will hit you as hard, if not harder, than it did me."

"Angie and Zane are *not* divorcing. He'll get over the puppies' digging frenzy. He loves Angie and she loves him." She typed in the code to open Jacob's unique gate. The red, one-of-a-kind, geometrically-shaped gate smoothly swung backward as if it were floating on air. The spectacular gate stood as mild foreplay to Jacob's award-winning, modern-designed mansion. "I'll swing by and talk to Angie after work. This is the last rule I'm breaking for you. We have five weeks left in our contracts. Stop fabricating problems between my friends." She drove forward and glanced in the rearview mirror as the gate closed behind her. "And I want documentation of our supposed marital status. I am tired of games."

"Zane has the photo. Ask him about it. I'm not lying. I wouldn't lie about loving you or marriage or Angie having terminal cancer."

"Jacob, it's like I don't know you anymore. You were never into me and now all of a sudden you are. You tell me you love me, but I don't know that you even know what love is." She drove forward over the long, winding road, ignoring his loud frustrations until the last of his words sank in. *Angie. Terminal. Cancer.*

She hit the brakes in front of his house and faced him. Her expression must have explained her shock because he started talking again before she could open her mouth to speak.

"She's seven months pregnant. She lost so much weight that the baby makes her look normal. The baby is struggling. Angie wears braces on her legs to help her walk more normally. She's done so much to prolong the image of healthy that when I saw her in her pajamas with no makeup and her wig off, I was stunned. I hadn't known she'd been wearing fake hair." His eyes filled with tears and it took him several swallows to continue. "She's been battling for her life all alone, knowing something was wrong, but not having confirmation until a couple of days before my accident. They thought it was all because of the pregnancy." He explained Zane and Angie's journey to now, and the path to an unknown future ahead of them.

"Who knows about her illness?" Sophia asked.

"Me, Lis, Blake, and you. There is a lot to do and not much time to do it."

"Um, Okay." She put the car in park and helped him inside. In a daze, she passed by the butler and maids and the chef, as she helped Jacob to his bedroom. "There has to be something doctors can do."

Jacob sat on the bed.

She stood between his legs and curled her arms

around his neck, holding him.

"I talked to Nathaniel Griffin's mom. She looked over the medical records. There is nothing anyone can do," Jacob whispered. "We aren't the ones who are ultimately in control. Bad things happen, often in succession. We're going get through this. We're going to be the friends they need us to be."

"I love you," she whispered.

"I love you more," he said. "This is your home now."

"You're my home, Jacob. Not this place."

"Well, then, go to work. Get your cupcakes baked and prepped and whatever it is you do in the mornings. Then come home to me."

She kissed him on the top of his head. "I'm going to stop by Angie and Zane's and cook for them. I need the show to tell me I can move in with you. I can't afford anymore fines." She wasn't sure how she was going to get through the morning without breaking down into a hot mess, but she didn't have a choice. She had to work. Hudson put his faith in her business sense and baking ability. "When I get the okay from the show, I'll call you, not a minute before."

She pushed everything away as she trudged through the house and out to her car. She started the engine and the phone rang. *Zane.*

"Hi, Zane," she answered. *Do I tell him I know? Do I ask him how he is?*

"Yesterday, I forgot to order cupcakes for Angie for today. Do you have time to make her those protein cupcakes she loves?" Zane asked.

"Of course. I'll have them delivered as soon as they're baked. I'm going to come over and cook dinner for you and Angie tonight. Anymore requests?" She tried to sound as chipper as she could.

"That would be great, Sophia. So great. Do you think you could stay for a while and visit after dinner?"

"Of course. You need some of Sophia's fabulousness?" She tried to keep it light. If they had a heart-to-heart, she would have to pull over and ugly cry. She'd never make it to the bakery to fulfill all the orders that had to be delivered today, and her stellar reputation would be trashed. A new business like hers wouldn't recover.

"To put it bluntly, yes. We need your sunshine, sparkles, and rainbows for a few hours."

"Color me there, Mr. Winslow. Tell my best friend her cupcakes will arrive warm and gooey and delicious very, very soon." *And then we'll cry together and figure out how on earth we're going to make the most of every day you have left.*

CHAPTER TWELVE

Jacob

SURPRISING SOPHIA AT WORK PROBABLY wasn't the best idea Jacob ever had. But he'd been left with few options, considering that her idea of taking care of him had been to send Hudson and Mr. and Mrs. Fox over to his house after work while Sophia spent her time with Angie, Zane, and their kids. He didn't need Hudson or the Foxes to help him. He had a full-time house staff to cook dinner, clean, and run errands. He needed his wife. As soon as he worked things out with the legal team at Pussy Pleasures, he'd have his wife at home and not battling fines.

Asking Blake to take him to the bakery resulted in Lis driving her pink girlie truck with her dog Bash sitting between her and Jacob, guarding her. With Lis as the defender of all women and dogs and whatever she considered "in need," Jacob regretted not calling a car service. If he had to hear what a fuckup he was one more time, he would lose his shit on her. She might be Zane's girl bestie and pregnant with triplets, but Jacob had Zane's back long before Lis came along. If anyone would support Zane through good times and bad, it was him.

"This is a bad call, Jacob. Bad. As in, the *worst*. You still haven't produced the marriage license. She's not slept in your bed or in your house." Lis slowed as they neared the bakery. "She doesn't trust you. Don't show up thinking you can help her when you look like you got hit by a truck, and you did. You're a damn ugly mess."

He had a copy of the marriage license and certificate in his back pocket. He might look like a pile of horse shit, but he wasn't spending one more night without her. "Thank you for bringing me."

"I'll wait outside. I doubt you'll be inside long," she said. She swiveled abruptly and Bash shifted, facing him. "Please don't go in there and try to take over. Hudson is the strong-and-silent type. It's sexy. Really sexy. Blake is like you. He goes in and takes over. He controls and dominates. It's sexy too, but sometimes it's a bit much." She inhaled and Bash leaned against her. The dog gazed up at her and nuzzled her neck, then gave Jacob an accusing stare as if Jacob needed to apologize to Lis. "Sophia needs a soft place to land, Jacob. Be that soft place so Hudson doesn't have another way to take Sophia from you. Don't order her."

"Thanks for the advice, Lis."

"Thank Bash, too," Lis demanded.

Jacob rolled his eyes at her. "Thank you, Bash. You're a great dog."

The dog turned his focus back to Lis, as if the apology wasn't worth his time.

Lis frowned. "He's sensitive, Jacob. You don't get that, do you? You're the only one who can throw a fit and be passionate about everything and everybody. Bash is passionate. He also calls bullshit when he sees it."

"He's a dog, Lis. *He's a dog.*"

She covered Bash's ears. "He's more than a dog. He has feelings, Jacob. Go and get your heart stomped on some more. Then maybe you'll get some sympathy from Bash. Until then, stop being an asshole to my dog."

Jacob held his tongue and opened the car door. He was still a little off-kilter from the accident, but he was well enough to go into work. No driving for two more weeks. Lis seemed to enjoy driving him places because whenever he called Blake for a ride, Lis showed up with Bash.

"One more thing," Lis said.

One more thing is always three more things with you. He turned. "Yes?"

"Pick up my order of a dozen cupcakes. If you end up staying longer than ten minutes, bring me the cupcakes." She placed her hand over her big, baby belly. "Don't be an asshole." She tilted her head down and stared at him. "You tend toward being an ass when things aren't going your way."

"Thanks for the pep talk, Lis. I can always count on you for that." He turned around.

"You're welcome," she shouted, then mumbled, "Asshole."

He kicked the car door closed with his heel and tried not to lean more to the right than the left as he walked toward the entrance. Immediately, he met Hudson's gaze.

Hudson walked around the counter and over to the door. He opened it. "Hey, Jake. Good to see you moving around so well."

Don't call me Jake. "It's Jacob, and thanks." He strode inside and followed the delicious scent of chocolate and raspberry to the counter. "Where's Sophia?"

"She took my mom and dad to the airport. I had a feeling you'd stop by, and I wanted to talk to you alone." Hudson turned the *open* sign over to *closed.*

"Blake called you?"

"Lis."

"Ahh," Jacob said. "I should have known. I am not her favorite person."

"She likes you. Everyone likes you. I wish I didn't like you." Hudson passed him on the way to the counter. A white box filled with cupcakes was wrapped up with a bow. He picked it up. "Let's walk out the front and give these to Lis."

"Are you expecting Sophia to stay with you tonight?" *I bet you are. You swooped in and gave her a safe place while I made mistake after mistake.*

Hudson walked and talked as they closed the shop and then made their way to Lis's sparkly pink truck.

"Sophia is staying with me for four more weeks. It's non-negotiable. It doesn't matter what you show her or what you say. I don't care if you're married to her or not, she's staying with me. I do not want another partner for the bakery. Sophia is the heart and soul of this shop, and I'll be damned if you fuck that up for either one of us. So, if you come sniffing around here for a taste of Sophia, the only person tasting her until the game is over is me." Hudson opened up the passenger side door of Lis's truck.

Lis's gaze fell straight to the box. She made a guttural, growling-moan. "Hand them over, Austin."

"Fort Worth, all your favorites are in here." Hudson stepped back and looked at Jacob. "Good talk. Call your staff if you need help around the house, not Sophia. I doubt you'll need that now, though. You seem to be getting around just fine."

You two have nicknames for each other? Is that a Texas thing? He climbed into the cab and buckled in. "You're not keeping me from my girl."

"Just did." Hudson said and closed the door.

Lis laughed. "He shut you down hard, Jacob. I think you met your match."

"I think I need a fucking cupcake." He used his cast to support the box as he untied the bow and opened the lid. "Which one is your favorite?"

"Hand over the chocolate ganache," Lis said.

Jacob picked it up and bit into it. "Oops. Is this the one you wanted?" He chewed and swallowed, then put the rest of it back in the box.

"That was not nice. I should kick your ass out of my truck."

"Well, what *you* did wasn't nice at all." He opened the car door and got out with the box of cupcakes.

"Get in the truck, Jacob," Lis said. "Give me that cupcake and look in the box to see which one you would like *most.*"

Bash barked, as if to emphasize Lis's order.

The dog looked like he would chase Jacob down and drag him back to the car, if Jacob decided to disobey. Bash seemed a lot like Jacob's dog Mistress Bark, only Mistress Bark had some maturity on the pup.

"Fine," Jacob said. He climbed into the cab and closed the door.

Bash scooted closer to Jacob and pushed his nose against the box on Jacob's lap.

Lis held her hand out for the cupcake he'd taken a bite out of. She snapped her fingers. "Babies need some sugar."

He handed her the partially eaten cupcake and then looked in the box. Under the spot where the chocolate ganache cupcake had been was Sophia's writing. He took out the vanilla raspberry cupcake to the right of the writing.

Lis held out her hand. "Another please. I want the one you're holding. You better not bite into it. It is *mine*."

He placed it in her hand.

"Give Bash the peanut butter one with the cookie in the shape of a bone. That one is a dog-safe cupcake. There's another one for Mistress Bark, but I think Bash deserves it more at the moment."

"If you weren't pregnant—"

"But I am, so *hand over another cupcake.* I need enough energy to deal with you and drive." She snapped her fingers again. "Hurry up. It's not good to keep a pregnant woman waiting."

He handed her a cupcake and the words written underneath the cupcakes began to form sentences. He took out the other dog cupcake and held it for Bash.

The grunts and squeaky moans Lis and Bash made while they inhaled their treats almost made Jacob laugh.

Jacob glanced at the two of them and two happy, satisfied smiles met his. "That good?"

"None better."

Bash seemed to agree with Lis and leaned over and licked her cheek and then shifted toward Jacob and kissed his cheek.

"He forgives you for being an asshole," Lis said.

Jacob sighed and looked into the box.

Jacob,

Hudson had one of his friends search for our marriage records. He found them and I now have a copy. I now know Zane was behind the contracts and the show. The director told me that if either one of us break one more rule, they will annul our marriage, and take my half of the bakery, and they wouldn't sell it back to me for five years. I'm staying with Hudson until the show calls for the reveal or fail, so I don't break the rules. I'm cooking dinner for Angie and Zane. Please don't come. Cook lunch for them. Maybe you can teach Zane some kitchen skills. That would ease Angie's mind. She's so worried about him. I'll leave notes for you with Angie or Lis. You can leave notes for me with them, too. Four weeks will go by fast.

Yours always,
Sophia.

How did it get to this? I need you with me. You know we're married, but you have the damn bakery on the Pussy Pleasures' poker table. Why did you allow that as part of the show's contract? He exhaled and felt the world crashing down around him. *You never thought I loved you. You never thought I would be the billionaire stranger on the show. You didn't believe in me, and I gave you no reason to believe in me.*

"How is that wedding cake cupcake?" Lis asked.

Jacob looked down at his hand. He hadn't realized he had eaten half of the white cake with white frosting and edible sugar pearls. "Delicious." Jacob closed the lid and put it on the floor between his feet.

Bash laid down with his head on Jacob's lap, seemingly sympathizing with his despair.

"Let's go to Zane's and pick up your dog and a few of the puppies," Lis said.

"Sounds good," Jacob said. "I'm sorry about being an asshole."

"It's okay. Sophia is safe. Kellen will be convicted and locked away for the rest of his life. That wouldn't have happened if you weren't so insanely in love with Sophia. Give her this time to focus on her bakery. She needs to do this herself. She has to trust her instincts and she needs to do it without your input. Hudson won't sabotage her. He loves her enough to help her thrive personally and professionally. Think about *her* and what *she needs from you.* Give her some space to soar and she will fly back to you. Send her reminders of how much you love her. She will be faithful. She won't disappoint you. So, *don't. Disappoint. Her.*"

Jacob stroked along Bash's back as he listened to Lis. He wanted to cry he missed Sophia so much. He wanted her with him. He...*This isn't about me.*

I need to take Andy's advice and remove myself from the equation until the contractual obligations are completed. Love is the ultimate goal, nothing else matters. I need to make sure Sophia keeps the business she worked so hard to get. Once we're finally together, I'll teach her the ins and outs of contracts and to never, ever, leave something so important vulnerable to a takeover.

"I'll make sure she's protected, even from my selfishness."

"You quit talking like that or I might just start to love you, too," Lis said.

Jacob huffed. He rolled his eyes at her. "Like that will ever happen." He chuckled. "Start driving. I've got to make Zane's day and take home all his puppies."

"Like that would be a hardship for you or Mistress Bark."

Jacob continued petting Bash as Lis began the drive to their neighborhood. *I've got to protect Sophia's business and renegotiate her contracts with Pussy Pleasures.* He'd do whatever needed to be done, even if it meant not seeing her for a while.

CHAPTER THIRTEEN

SOPHIA

KNEELING BESIDE ANGIE'S BEDSIDE IN the guest room she used to sleep in at Angie and Zane's house, Sophia silently prayed for miraculous healing.

Thin, bony fingers uncurled between the metal rails of the hospital bed Zane had bought for her. "Hold my hand," Angie whispered.

The end was near; Sophia felt her best friend slipping away more and more each day. She carefully placed her hand over Angie's. "Do you need anything?"

"You to be pregnant and happy with Jacob."

I need that, too. "Did he leave a note this week?" It had been four weeks with no contact. *Why hasn't he left a note, something? Lis and Angie would never say a word about it to the show.*

"No," Angie mumbled. "May God give you a baby boy to love and me to live long enough to hear your good news."

"You're going to hear it, Angie. You'll be the first person I tell."

"My baby isn't going to make it," Angie mumbled. "Help Zane when I'm gone. Find him someone. Someone who he will love more than me. Someone who will never take him for granted, never cheat on him out of anger. Someone whose passion for life is contagious."

"He forgave you for that one time," Sophia said. "Don't do this, Angie. Don't beat yourself up over one indiscretion. You don't have to pray for him to love someone more than you. Just stop it."

"I do," Angie said. "He blames himself for what I'd done. It wasn't him. It was me. I was scared. I pushed him away. I told him I didn't love him, that I'd never love him. I think he believed me. I think he still believes those words I said in anger four years ago."

"No, he doesn't," Sophia said. "He doesn't. He knows you love him with all your heart."

"No, he doesn't. He never has, but I do. I love him so much that I want him to be with someone who will show him she loves him. Someone whose heart sings when he's around. Someone who soothes his hurts, heals his soul, always speaks the truth. I want him to know love without any strings attached. Pray with me, now."

Sophia's heart broke apart for her friend. Her stomach knotted and twisted until she thought she might get sick. The secrets that Angie had hid from her all these years, the worries, the fears, the truth of her heart found a strong voice today.

Sophia closed her eyes and prayed for her best friend to find peace and for Zane to love again. And selfishly, she prayed for Jacob to send her a sign, a note, something to reassure her he still loved her.

CHAPTER FOURTEEN

JACOB

WATCHING ZANE DOWN ANOTHER SHOT of whiskey in the kitchen worried Jacob. Booze wasn't the answer, not long-term—which was the route Zane seemed most willing to take.

"Buddy, how about a cup of coffee?" Jacob walked over to the espresso machine in the kitchen and opened the cabinet where Zane kept the ground beans.

"No, man. I'm good. Coffee is Angie's thing. I don't think she even recognizes me anymore. She's so doped up."

The cabinet was empty of anything coffee related. Every day, Zane seemed to fall apart a little more. He started drinking as soon as the kids went to sleep and continued until Jacob helped him into bed.

"You can't continue to do this to yourself," Jacob said. "You've got kids to take care of." He walked to the island counter where Zane drowned his feelings and sat next to his best friend.

"I know. I know. I just need a little reprieve. She keeps asking for the newborn, not realizing she hasn't given birth. The baby doesn't have a heartbeat anymore. Nothing. It's as gone as she is going to be when she realizes she's lost what she was living for."

"Oh, man," Jacob mumbled. *I'd be drunk for a few days, too.* "I'm so sorry."

Zane lifted his glass up in what seemed like a toast. "My unborn child is dead. My wife is going to die. My kids will never know their mother. I'm a shitty father. I've never been a good dad. I'm as bad as my own father. Hell, I might be worse. He never drank when my mother died. He left me to the nanny to raise and went to work."

"Don't compare yourself to your father. He's changed a lot, and he is a wonderful grandfather. His wife is grandma central with the kids. She absolutely loves them. They are both there for you." *I wish you'd talk to your father. He went through the same thing only with a preteen, not toddlers.*

"Yeah, well I will. I am like my old man. My wife is crying out for some other dude to hold her. When Maddie Morgan comes over to care for Angie, my dick stands at attention. What does that make me? I'll tell you. It makes me the biggest sonofabitch in a roomful of them." Zane downed his drink and placed the glass on the table. "I don't think Angie loved me the way she loved that dude I paid off to leave her alone. He loved money, not her. And she loved him more than me. I pissed her off and she ran to him. Fucked him to spite me."

"Zane, she loved you. She made a mistake all

those years ago. She owned up to it. Now, she's not in her right mind. You can't take anything that she says right now as coming from her heart."

Zane shook his head. "You sound like Maddie. She said the same thing, but I think Maddie's fiancé said similar stuff at the end and it was the truth that hurt her. I don't know what kind of pain he caused her, but that girl has been through some serious emotional shit she won't talk about. And I want to fuck it out of her." He barked a disgusted-with-himself laugh. "I must be drunk because I think I just told you I wanted to fuck the little blonde spitfire of a nurse taking care of my wife."

"Dude, you're a drunk mess, that's for sure. Wanting and doing are two very different things. You're hurting, Zane. I've known you forever—trust me, you're one of the good guys."

"I feel like being good isn't worth it." Tears that seemed to come out of nowhere rolled down Zane's cheeks. "I love Angie. I love my kids. I want a miracle. I want that Maddie nurse to come in and tell me my wife is in remission. But that isn't in the cards. She's going to tell me it's time to go call in a physician. Then I'll never see Angie again. I'll never see the nurse who brings a ray of light that shines in this miserable house of death three days a week. I'll raise two kids without the woman I pledged my heart, soul, and body to love for as long as we both lived. I'm never going to fall in love again. I hate love. I hate everything about love."

Jacob hugged his best friend. "You're allowed to hate everything right now, but it won't always be like this."

Zane's body trembled as he cried. "I need her and she's already gone."

There were no words of solace Jacob could muster. Angie's fight for life would be over soon. Maddie would move on to her next job. Zane would raise his kids as a single parent with the help of his close friends.

"Forget what I said about Maddie. I didn't mean it. I just don't—"

"It's forgotten. You're hurting, Zane. Give yourself a little break when it comes to Maddie. She's a beautiful woman and you're a guy who hasn't had sex in more than six months. It's a natural reaction. Just don't act on it."

"I'd never act on it. I need to go to bed and never drink again." Zane leaned against Jacob.

"Let's get you to bed, and tomorrow, no alcohol."

Zane nodded. "I promise no more alcohol."

"I'm holding you to it," Jacob said. *And I'm calling your dad tonight. You need him, even if you won't admit you do.*

"I'm going to get you and Sophia on Pussy Pleasures tomorrow. No more waiting. Love wins, Jacob. I want love to win for someone. I want love to win for you."

Jacob caught Zane as he tried to stand but promptly stumbled to the side. "I got you, big guy. Let's get you to bed."

"Thanks, man. I can always count on you." Zane leaned on Jacob as they made their way to the bedroom.

Jacob tucked Zane into bed and checked on the kids. As soon as Zane began to snore softly, he snuck into Angie's room and saw Maddie Morgan sitting by the bedside holding Angie's hand.

"How's she doing?" Jacob whispered.

"Won't be long," Maddie said. "Zane is the one I'm worried about. He is taking everything Angie says to heart. She calls for him. He comes and she starts to babble about someone else and cry. It's breaking him."

"He's going to get through this. I think he's going to stop drinking in the evenings."

"That's a start," Maddie said. "I hope he and Angie have a moment. Something to help him find closure and peace."

"Me, too. He doesn't give his heart to anyone easily, but once he does, it's theirs forever. She has his."

She nodded. "He's one of those prince charming types. You're one, too. Whatever you and Sophia are going through, I know you two will come out stronger and more in love than ever. She has a baby bump now, although she hasn't said anything about being pregnant. Could you be the father?" She gazed up. Her pretty summer blue eyes, full of life, brightened the room.

He nodded. "If she's pregnant, I am most definitely the father."

Sparkles of light shined in her eyes. "I thought so. Do you want me to tell her anything?"

"No messages. I'll be with her soon. Two days to be exact. Then we will never be apart again."

"Be sure to remind her you love her more with each passing day," Maddie said. "Don't keep it inside. Tell her."

"Yes, ma'am. You're a smart lady. And thanks for caring for Angie and Zane. I'm heading home now." He turned to go.

"I'm not smart, Mr. Bell. I've learned through loss and bearing the cross of a broken heart. I'm in this field to ease the pain of patients and help those going through what I have to understand the process and find closure. Be safe, and have a good night. Hopefully our paths will cross again, but during a happier time."

With new compassion for the nurse whose brother gave him the best advice he'd gotten in a long time, he turned around. "I consider you and your brother friends. I expect to see you often over the years, and for you to celebrate with me and Sophia as our family expands. I also expect to celebrate with you and your brother when you find love and have a family of your own."

She shook her head. "Love is not for me. A baby, maybe?" She shrugged. "Maybe not."

As he watched her look over at Angie and then the photo of Zane and the kids, he saw a longing in her gaze. *You want a family. I need to set you up with Hudson. He wants a family and I need to get him to forget about my wife. He's a good guy. You're a sweet woman. I'm going to get Lis to get you on Pussy Pleasures. No. Damn. You almost got married. No way you're a virgin.*

"Call me if you need me." *As soon as I have Sophia in my bed at home, I'm going to talk to Hudson about Maddie. They'd be a good match.*

"Will do," she answered.

He strode out of the room and out of the house. *Two days until I see my wife again. Two days until I find out if Maddie is correct in assuming that belly bump is a baby.*

CHAPTER FIFTEEN

SOPHIA

HANGING UP HER APRON, SOPHIA closed her eyes for a second, preparing for the emotional trip to see her best friend. *Please be lucid when I'm there, Angie. Please come back to us for just a little while.*

Hudson came up behind her and wrapped his arms around her waist. "Where are we going tonight?"

He asked that every evening when he arrived to pick her up. He seemed to always know what she needed. He kept her on a tight schedule and, with his support and help, she managed to get through the day without having an ugly cry or meltdown over slowly losing her best friend, missing her dog, and being forced to stay away from Jacob.

She turned around in his arms and curled her arms around his chest. "Angie's house. Did you wrap up the boxes for them?"

"Yes, ma'am. They're in my truck. Haus is in the back guarding them."

"Not Jacob's today? It's been more than seven

weeks," Hudson said.

She snuggled closer to him and pressed her cheek against his chest. *Not until I get the call from Pussy Pleasures for the pregnancy reveal or fail.* "Not today."

"Are you avoiding him? Are you considering annulling your marriage? Are you going to tell him about the pregnancy?" Hudson asked.

"I don't know what I'm doing," she mumbled. *I've written notes to him every day and given them to Lis or Angie to pass along. He hasn't sent a note, flower, or text. When Jacob moves on, he moves on.* "I figured he might ask how I was feeling or if I was having symptoms of a pregnancy. He hasn't. And there is no proof I'm pregnant, just a few mild symptoms."

"Puking in the morning, every morning, is more than a mild symptom. And you're curvier everywhere. And I think it's time for a test for confirmation so you'll stop fighting me on shopping for maternity clothes."

"My curves are from eating too many cupcakes, not pregnancy."

He shook his head and huffed a lighthearted laugh. "Whatever you want to think is fine with me, but soon your shirts aren't going to cover your belly and you're going to have to come to the realization that you're pregnant."

She rolled her eyes. "Okay, Hudson. You made your point for the hundredth time."

"Finally you're seeing things my way. Are you considering my proposal?" Hudson asked. "I love you and the little one I am sure you're carrying."

Hard cock pressed against her belly. Every day

she came closer to giving in to her fears that Jacob had forgotten about her and the baby she came closer to believing was growing inside her. Bouts of morning sickness and tender breasts added to the reasons behind Hudson's declaration of her pregnant status. He didn't tell anyone, but when they were alone, he asked about her and how she was doing. He'd even bought a book about what to expect while she was pregnant, and he read it to her each week. Hudson was wonderful, but she wanted Jacob, and that desire hadn't waned at all. The yearning to be reunited with Jacob actually grew, day by day. Every time she felt Hudson's hot body pressed against hers, she wished it was Jacob. She wanted forever with her billionaire ex-boss. She wanted a family. She wanted a puppy she and Jacob chose together. A puppy she felt Rufus would be proud to watch over from Heaven.

"I am considering your offer, but there would be issues I'm not ready to talk about. Not yet. Not until I deal with Jacob, if he ever decides to talk to me again." She hadn't quite told him the truth, but she hadn't lied either.

Not telling Hudson about Pussy Pleasures had been difficult but he didn't push for her to confide in him. He didn't push her to see Jacob and clear the air. She had signed up with the show for a baby, not a husband. If Hudson was right, she would get her baby. But Hudson believed she would get her heart's desire. Only, her heart desired Jacob, not him. She put her signature on so many contracts stating she'd spread her legs on the live-stream as many times as her Billionaire 43 wanted her to. Thinking about being on that set with Jacob again got her so damn hot between her thighs that all Hudson would have to do is slide his hand between her legs and she'd come hard. She held in the moan rising in her throat. If Jacob were there, he would have had his hands down her pants, finding only flesh and no panties. Before she knew what he was doing, she'd be crying out in bliss from an epic orgasm.

She inhaled as her heart sped a billion miles a minute.

Jacob would make that rough, angry-but-aroused noise he made when he was…*Jacob, I need you.*

"Sophia, stop doing that," Hudson mumbled.

She gazed up at him and his eyes weren't the hazel eyes she yearned to see. His body wasn't the one she wanted to be holding. "I'm sorry." She backed away.

Her phone rang.

He slipped his hand into the pocket of her apron hanging on the hook nearby. "Sugar, you're not yourself today." He pulled out her phone and handed it to her.

"Hello?" she answered.

"Sophia Richland Bell?" Evan, the director at Pussy Pleasures, asked.

"Yes, sir. That's me." She opened the door to the back room and exited into the parking lot behind the building. Hudson followed, quickly switching places and opening and locking the doors.

"I thought so, but had to make sure. It's Evan from Pussy Pleasures. It's time to schedule your appointment with Dr. Bledwell. Have you taken a pregnancy test yourself?"

"No, I haven't," she said. She hadn't been sure

that an over-the-counter test was in the contract, and she wasn't about to chance it. Even with Hudson's belief that she was pregnant, he hadn't pushed for a test to confirm their suspicions. And between the bakery and visiting Angie, she hadn't done anything for herself besides cling to Hudson at night.

"Well, you made it this far. Is there going to be a question as to who the father might be?" Evan asked. "You've been living with another man and sleeping in his bed. Things have gotten heated between the two of you."

Hudson opened the door to the passenger side of his truck and she stepped in.

She closed the door. "I've only been with Jacob. No one else. I did kiss the man I am living with, but that is it and it was before my marital status was verified."

"I'm sending a driver to Angie Winslow's house tonight at seven to pick you up for primping. Because your Billionaire 43 requested an extension of time to make up for breaking so many rules, and since both of you adhered to them without any incidents since the extension, I am pleased to tell you that the bonus special is now in effect. You'll find out more about that after this portion of the show is completed."

"I have to be at the bakery in the morning, early," she said. "I can't do it tonight."

"We have a team who will arrive at the bakery in the morning to assist you. They are yours for the next three months and will be paid by Pussy Pleasures," Evan said. "I'll see you in a few hours, Sophia."

"See you soon," she whispered. Cream frosted her pussy lips. *Jacob trusted me not to make love to Hudson. He didn't write because he couldn't. He worked a new deal to save my partnership in the bakery.*

Hudson climbed into the driver's seat. "Zane's?"

She nodded. "I can't marry you," she whispered.

"Think about it a little longer," Hudson said. "We don't know what Jacob has planned. You might find you like strong and steady instead of overzealous and unpredictable."

She nodded. He had a valid point, but he didn't know Jacob on a day-to-day basis like she did. Jacob was passionate, encouraging, motivating, intense, loyal, loving, fair, and honest. He had a wild streak, but he wasn't vindictive. He protected the ones he loved any way he could because he knew loss, lots of loss. Most of all, he knew how to get through the hard times, and help others get through them, too.

CHAPTER SIXTEEN

JACOB

STRETCHING HIS ARMS OVERHEAD, JACOB stared in the mirror at his body. His left arm had lost some muscle mass because of the cast, but he had gained enough back in the last couple weeks of rehab that he looked fairly symmetrical. His abs had never looked so good. His cock seemed to be bigger and stronger, probably from jerking off multiple times a day, as he neared the end of their agreement with the show. He and Zane and the legal department had reworked the contracts both he and Sophia had signed. Sophia had signed her life away to Pussy Pleasures, and getting all those revisions took more time and effort than Jacob had ever imagined.

Evan peeked his head into the dressing room. "Ready to see her?"

Jacob's cock jerked at the mention of seeing his wife. "Yeah, man. It's been eight weeks without any contact. I'm more than ready." *Thirteen weeks since I made love to her. I'm ready to carry her over the threshold of my house and shower her with love every day of her life.*

"Then come on." Evan opened the door. "She's waiting, and the amount of comments on the live-stream are gonna get us both extra bonuses in our contracts."

With his colored contacts in and his mask secured, Jacob walked down an aisle of bright lights toward the set.

"As soon as you see the camera backing away from her pussy, you can go in and get her." Evan stepped to the side.

With her wrists and ankles strapped to poles bolted to the floor and extended to the ceiling, Sophia moaned and writhed on a covered mat on the floor. Her pussy was soaked with juices and her clit and nipples were clamped, waiting for him.

With each step closer, the raw need to have her, claim her, and never let her go took over.

He dropped to his hands and knees between her legs and dove in, licking, tasting, feasting on her. He slid down the small metal ring holding the silicone-tipped clamps in place, taking control and lessening the pressure.

Her pussy quivered. Her legs trembled. The sexy squeak she made had him thinking of getting his cock in her immediately, but he dipped his tongue inside her and squeezed the small tong-like pieces together in a milking motion.

"Yes," she screamed. Yanking against the cuffs, she bucked but he knew what he was doing. He'd done it time and time before with women who were new to toy experimentation. With his experience, he planned to reward her for her fidelity. She'd had so many opportunities with Hudson and hadn't taken them. He'd seen the private moments in Hudson's bed. He'd seen her so close, but always pulling back, retreating.

Juices gushed into his mouth. He lapped and lapped, then took the clamp off and threw it away from them. Leisurely, he laved over her pussy and mons, taking time to trace the Kitten 43 tattoo before nuzzling and licking his way upward to the sensual clips at her breasts. A kiss here. A swirl of his tongue there.

He rolled his fingers over her nipples and the length of the clamps, loosening them—one, and then the other—playing with the pressure until she arched her back and her juices kissed his cock that was begging to start claiming his woman with his cum.

"Fuck me. Please. Fuck me," she begged.

"Not yet," he whispered.

She pulled against the restraints, arched her back and whimpered as he slid the small ring toward the top of the clamps, increasing the pressure.

She drew in a sharp breath.

"Too much?" he whispered.

Her chest rose and fell in labored breaths as she shook her head from side to side. "No. Oh. Fuck. No."

"More?" he whispered.

He lessened the pressure and thrust his pelvis. Her juices coated his cock as he entered her, but she was tight.

So.

Damn.

Tight.

One quick release and he tossed the clamps to

the floor away from them and grunted as he thrust.

She gasped as he buried his cock deep within her.

He retreated without saying a word, taking in her beauty as his gaze drifted over her.

Her breasts seemed larger, fuller, and when she shifted from side to side, the movement seemed extra salacious, like she'd done this before, like she knew how much he wanted her and knowing it made her bold and demanding. It could have been his imagination, but she seemed more comfortable in her body, more confident.

Her pussy gripped his cock and he was done holding back. He glided his smooth and oiled chest over her big breasts, and down. Once his cock slipped out, he powered into her again, gliding his body upward, rubbing against her chest. Sliding his hands between her body and the soft linens, he gripped her hips.

Over and over. Again and again. Up and down.

Faster. Faster. Stronger thrusts. Harder grinds.

Down and up over her soft feminine curves.

Down and up.

Out and in.

Out and in.

The mumbling and screaming jumble of moans culminated in a wild frenzy of hungry roars.

"Mine. Mine. Mine," he shouted.

Her body coiled and released in a flurry of shudders. His release came right after. He spurted inside her and pulled out and pumped his cock with his hand, spurting her clit and breasts and belly with his cum, and then thrust into her one more time to finish her off.

He grinned as he gazed into her eyes. "I love you."

"Wow," Evan's voice interrupted Jacob. "Let's get Kitten 43 cleaned up for the doctor. Absence does make the heart grow fonder, or maybe it makes the reunion that much sexier."

"It does both," Sophia said.

"Billionaire 43, we're sending you away for a few minutes," Evan said. "Don't go far because your job here is not done."

I really hate dealing with your commentary, Evan.

"And we're on break. Lover 43, let's get you out of here. We need to set up the next scene."

Four women and two men came through doors on either side of the three-walled room and before he realized what was happening, Jacob was led off the set into a shower room for bathing and extra polishing.

"Are you doing this to my wife?" he asked one of the girls.

"Yes, sir," she answered. "Everything we do to you, she is getting the equivalent for a female."

He nodded. "Does she like all the waxing and scrubs?"

"Yes, sir. She does. You can encourage her to continue the regime we've set. She can come to our exclusive spa. It's lovely. Most of the Kittens from our shows come twice a month. I can set her up on a schedule."

"Do that."

"We can do the same for you," she said.

He nodded. "Schedule us together." *I'm going to give my wife everything she ever wanted, and everything she never knew she wanted.*

CHAPTER SEVENTEEN

SOPHIA

STRAPPED DOWN TO A SEX bench with her belly and chest against the cushion and her ass higher than her head, Sophia couldn't believe the turn of events. Jacob made love to her on the first segment of the show like she'd dreamed he would—gentle and rough, taking his time and working his way across every inch of her body.

He loved her even though she'd had several moments with Hudson that almost turned to sex, but didn't. He'd renegotiated her contracts, saved her bakery from being taken over by Pussy Pleasures, and worked his vast network to help the prosecution build a rock-solid case against the serial killer Kellen Pruitt. Two other women Kellen had stalked were saved because of Rufus's powerful bite marks, placing Kellen in her apartment and his blood mixed with her dog's, and because Kellen chose the wrong man to crash into. Jacob was stronger, smarter, and had family guardian angels protecting him. Jacob and Rufus had saved not only her life, but the lives of other women who were unlucky enough to meet the man with the three-inch dick.

Jacob kissed the side of her cheek. "Are you still with me?"

"Yes, sir," she whispered. "Sorry."

He nuzzled her neck. "Hey, I don't care if you're pregnant or not. Whatever the tests show, know I will love you for the rest of my life. Nothing will ever change that."

The doctor told you I'm not pregnant. I should have taken a test. I should have made sure I was pregnant. All hope drained from her body as her heart broke into tiny pieces. All that *morning sickness had been my nerves, not symptoms of pregnancy. The breast tenderness could be hormonal. Missing my period had to have been because of stress. This show gave me the best chance at getting pregnant. I should have produced a billion eggs ready to be fertilized, but I didn't. I produced a small number of eggs and most of them probably weren't viable. Not even Jacob Bell, super sperm man, could get me pregnant.*

She forced a smile as her chin dropped farther over the end of the bench. *After all the challenges of the last few months, I want this reward. I want a baby we can celebrate. I want Rufus to bark with joy on the other side of the rainbow, and to watch over us and our baby. Because of him, and you, I'm still here.*

So many obstacles had been in their way, yet they were on Pussy Pleasures, making love as husband and wife. Sure, there were millions watching via live-stream, but she found pleasure in knowing she was the star of the show and the audience wanted a happily ever after as much as she did.

With her own and Angie's prayers every day for her to become pregnant, she had to have a chance at it. Giving Angie a reason to smile and celebrate would mean the world to Sophia. They had spent years wishing to be pregnant at the same time, dreaming of raising their kids together, of growing old as soul sisters. Now, it looked like none of those dream would come true.

"Sweetheart, what's wrong?"

"Nothing," she whispered. *I want your baby.*

He growled. "Wrong answer. Tell me."

She shrugged a little. "Nothing. Really." *They never should have accepted my application into this program. They never should have taken a chance on me and my faulty reproductive system.*

"Nothing, huh?" He stood up and slid the palm of his hand along the length of her back to the curve of her ass.

"Truly, nothing. I'm fine." *Sad. Disappointed. Scared. You want a family. I'll have to go through more fertility treatments that probably won't work. We'll have to look at other options. I don't want to have to get a surrogate to give us a baby. I don't want someone else carrying your child. I want to feel every stage of growth. I want to—*

Thwack.

She gasped as her bottom burned with the unexpected spank. "*What* was that?"

"Testing the new paddles," he said without any inflection. "You're fine?"

Her ears perked up for an order or a change in

his tone.

Silence.

"I am fine," she said. *You do not need to hear all the fears I've built up over the course of our separation.*

Thwack.

She tensed. "Seriously, nothing is wrong." *I love you. I want us to have a baby. I've been an emotional hot mess. I've missed you and want us to have a child. My best friend is dying. The baby she's carrying...too much tragedy. I want to bring Angie something to celebrate before she passes on.*

"Kitten, you protest too much."

Thwack. Thwack. Thwack.

Thwack, thwack, thwack.

She gripped the handle attached to the leg of the bench. *You're going to chastise me for being disappointed and not telling you? I haven't seen you in eight weeks and you're upset I'm not baring my soul to you? My best friend is dying. Dying. Asshole.*

"I like this one," he said.

"Yeah," resounded from the filming crew. "Paddle that ass."

"One more chance to tell the truth." The warning seemed to hover over her like a search and rescue helicopter. "What is wrong?" Jacob ordered more than asked.

After all the waiting, all the worry, all the trust I lived with for the last eight weeks, you're demanding that I tell you I'm terrified I'll never be able to get pregnant in front of the world? "Nothing is wrong. Absolutely. *Nothing.*"

"Oh, my sweet kitten." He sighed. "Trust is essential in a relationship. Do you trust me?"

Her heartbeat skyrocketed. "You know I do." *You're not going to—*

"So you trust me."

"Yes. Don't you trust me to tell you if something is wrong?" She wanted to look at him and the size of the paddle. She needed to see if his questioning was a way to send her off balance or if he intended to actually paddle her as punishment for not telling him her feelings. But if she did look, he *would* punish her for not trusting him to do what is best for her and their relationship. She knew the drill, his drill. Clothed or naked, the man worked the angles and punished when he felt he'd been wronged in some way.

"We'll start with three and see if the truth will come out."

Shit.

Thwack.

"Fuck you."

"I see we'll have to teach you a lesson," he said with a gravelly voice.

"You're turned on," she mumbled.

Thwack.

She gasped as her bottom cheeks lit on fire. She gripped the metal handles on the legs of the bench tighter than she had ever held anything. The heat penetrated into her muscles and instead of tears filling her eyes with a punishment, her pussy clenched and wanted the wide piece of wood to make contact again.

"The correct answer is 'One'."

Thwack.

The width landed hard on the lower portion of her bottom bordering her thighs. She squeaked and her eyes watered, but she held on and kept position. The fire burning her cheeks held a sting, but also held a promise that if she gave him what he wanted, pleasure would follow. "One."

Thwack.

Another squeak left her lips from the precise wielding of Jacob's paddle against her ass and cushioned her pussy. To her surprise, the initial spark of pain spread into her muscles and sent a surge of heat deep into her center. A raw, sexy moan spilled out as her channel walls squeezed and juices flowed over her folds. "Tha-ree."

Guttural groans and low-toned calls for more filled in the background noise.

His firm-yet-gentle palms massaged into her heated flesh and muscles of her hips.

"Not much of a punishment, was it?" he asked.

The more he caressed the stronger the unbearable need for his cock to tunnel into her center became. He had to have known she was seconds away from losing control, the way her juices continued to trickle down and tease her clit. She would come if his fingers grazed anywhere near her clit. If he pressed his cock to her, she was a goner.

Touch me. Jacob, touch me.

He chuckled. "I see it was enough. Tell me what upset you, and I'll give you a reward." He continued to massage her bottom, sliding his hands closer and closer to the girlie parts she needed touched.

"I..." *Fuck me.*

His fingers stopped at the tip of her opening near her clit. "Focus, Kitten."

Okay. Okay. The call for sex held such a powerful grip on her that her mouth opened and finally obeyed his order to tell him what was wrong. "I want a child and it may never happen. If I can't conceive, will you still want me?"

"I married *you,* not your uterus," he said. "I'd love to have children with you. If that doesn't happen, I've got you. You're enough. You, my beautiful bride, are plenty to keep me happy and satisfied for the rest of my life. Anything else is icing on the wedding cake."

The helmet of his cock entered her and pushed in farther. With the heated desire burning inside her and the steel rod of his cock burrowing deeper and deeper, she strained against the straps holding her arms and legs in position. She needed to push back, turn over and ride his cock, but she couldn't. She had to wait, to obey, to accept his domination and trust him like she did before all the doubts rushed back in. She had to revel in his pleasure, in his love, in his desire. She had to believe that no matter what happened, he would protect her, love her, and never, ever let her go again.

She moaned as his cock tapped her cervix. His balls, slick from her juices, hit flush against her blossomed clit. The pleasure rose. Her pussy contracted. Her clit trembled, ready to surrender to bliss. Love spiraled upward from within her soul and sang from her lips. "I love you."

He grunted louder and louder as he rocked back and plunged his cock in. In. In. He shifted side to side and foraged in her pussy, seemingly searching to make sure he found every nook and cranny of pleasure. His hands gripped her hips tighter.

He thrust.

In. Out.

In.

Out.

In.

In.

In.

Her belly contracted along with her pussy and ass.

"Fuck, yeah," he roared. He shuddered and the cum she wanted to feel inside her flowed, marking her as his.

The squeaks and noises of pleasure she made seemed to please him.

He withdrew too soon. Her orgasm continued on without him inside her.

"Oh, baby, I love you," Jacob whispered.

"Sorry to interrupt," Evan said. "Kitten 43, are you ready to find out the test results?"

Jacob's fingers glided up her inner thigh to her wet pussy lips and opened them. "But I'm not done." He shoved his fingers inside and out. In and out. In and out.

"Oh, God," she whimpered. "Oh, God. Yes."

Evan cleared his throat. "Couple 43 are about to find out the results of the tests."

"I get to be present during the results?" Jacob said.

"Yes, but she needs to be unstrapped. You can hold her," Dr. Bledwell said.

It's worse than I thought. They're afraid I'm going to lose it when they tell me I'm the first Virgin Kitten on the show who didn't get pregnant. I'm not going to freak out. Please, don't cry. She swallowed hard. *I can do this.*

Jacob's hand slid from her body.

The restraints on her thighs loosened and two sets of firm hands massaged her legs.

"I'm right here, love of my life," Jacob said. He released the ties holding her arms down and caressed up and down each arm. "I love you no matter what happens."

She closed her eyes and prayed that her fertility problems had miraculously disappeared and she was not only going home with her husband, but making a pit stop at her best friend's house to celebrate.

Jacob helped her up. The trickle of fluids down her thighs and the lovely sensitivity of her pussy as she moved her legs and stood gave her a deeper sense of desire for her husband. The lengths to which he went to repair the harm from the rules he'd broken in his contract proved without a doubt that he loved her.

He carried her to the red linens with white geometric shapes on the four poster bed. Every Virgin Kitten who had ever been on the show had a version of pink and blue flowered bedding during their reveal. She'd broken the pregnancy streak. That was the only reason she could think of for the change in linen colors. They took a chance on her and she had failed them. She failed Rufus. She failed Angie. And most of all, she'd failed Jacob.

He sat down and arranged the pillows behind him, then pulled her onto his lap.

She curled her arms around him and buried her face against his neck. *Please give me this one thing. Please. Let the morning sickness be real.*

Let this little baby Hudson and I have been talking to be real.

"Are you ready?" the doctor asked.

She crossed her fingers between Jacob's neck and the pillows so no one would see. "I guess so."

"The tests came back positive," Dr. Bledwell said.

She whipped her head around and faced him. "What?" *Did I hear you correctly?*

Dr. Bledwell grinned. "You're very pregnant."

"I'm pregnant?" She repeated the words over and over.

"She's pregnant?" Jacob asked as if he didn't believe it either.

"She is," the doctor said.

"So, I'm having a baby?" she asked. *Hudson was right. Oh my goodness, he was right.*

"No, ma'am. You're having two babies. The ultrasound confirmed them," Dr. Bledwell said.

"Them?" Jacob's hands on her belly felt cold and clammy on her skin.

"Congratulations, you're having twins," Evan shouted.

"Twins," Jacob mumbled, and pulled her closer.

"In about seven months, you two will be taking home two babies from the hospital," the doctor said.

She shifted and turned around in Jacob's lap. "We're going to..."

A smirk on his face told her he played her this whole time.

"You knew," she said.

He cradled the back of her head. "I didn't, but I had a feeling I could close the baby deal. Plus"—

he slid his hand over her belly—"this small curve wasn't there the last time I saw you." He kissed her softly.

Evan stepped in front of them. "For more about Kitten and Billionaire 43, check out the bonus footage and get ready for their live interview later tonight." Evan smiled. "That's a wrap."

"B. B., come," Jacob shouted.

Small squeaky barks and the tapping of toenails on wood came from behind the set and ended on the other side of the bed.

Jacob leaned over and brought up a bundle of light brown fur in the form of a mixed terrier puppy. "Meet Big B. He's following Mistress Bark's tutelage, but I have faith you will take over and stop him from making our house bark central."

She sat up and shifted onto her knees. She flung her arms around Jacob's neck and hugged him and their puppy. "You didn't have to—"

"He's never going to be Rufus, but he's going to be a great dog," Jacob said. "Angie showed me a pic of this little guy a few weeks ago, and I knew he was the one. He passed Mistress's approval, so…" Jacob blushed. "He's a cutie."

She kissed Jacob and took the puppy from him. *Those are some huge paws.* "He's going to be big."

"Yeah," Jacob said. "Big enough to handle the additions we'll be bringing home in seven months. And his heart is as big as his bark."

The pup calmed down as they held and petted him together.

"I already love him," she whispered. "Is it weird that I think Rufus had a hand in giving us this cute little guy?"

"No, baby. Mistress Bark has been sad until I showed her a photo of Big B. She did that funny dance when I introduced him to her like she did when you introduced Rufus to her. Dogs watch over us when they're here on earth or in Heaven. He sent us a puppy who needs to protect and love us, and at the same time gave us a puppy to protect and love." He shifted the puppy into her arms. "This little guy has Rufus's stamp of approval written all over him."

"I'm going to be the first one done with the shower and sitting in the interview chair," she said and sprinted off the set with the puppy in her hands. "I'm going to win."

"I won everything that mattered." He chased after her.

She stopped and waited for him. "What is that?"

He swept her up and carried her to her dressing room. "I won you. I didn't really win you, but I believed in you, that your heart was mine as mine is yours. And you taught me something."

"What?"

"Throwing money at a problem isn't always the answer. Sometimes, trusting in love, loyalty, kindness, and faithfulness is the only course of action to take when a person screws up and breaks every rule imaginable. I loved you enough to step away and fix my mistakes. But I'm never leaving you again." He kissed her. "You, Mrs. Jacob Bell, are the love and light of my life."

"I don't know what to say," she whispered.

He opened the door to her dressing room. "Don't say anything. Meet me in the interview room. I want to tell the world you're mine and then take you home and make love to you in the privacy of our bedroom. No more cameras for a while, okay?"

"I kind of like it," she said.

"How about we film ourselves making love and let the next Kitten find her perfect match here on the set?"

"Now, that sounds like a perfect plan," she said.

The End 

ALSO BY ANNA LORES

CONTEMPORARY ROMANCE
Billionaire 43
Billionaire 42
Ella's Triple Pleasure
The Horse List
The Horse List Challenge
The Horse List Unveiled

PARANORMAL ROMANCE
Cursed to Love
One Night of Love

For more steamy stories,
visit Anna at *www.AnnaLoresAuthor.com*

ABOUT THE AUTHOR

An avid romance reader, Anna Lores started writing steamy romance novels as a by-product of insomnia. One night, with a nudge from her husband to write a book, Anna borrowed her son's laptop and set about breathing life to her very own characters. After a month, she was surprised with a new laptop of her own to pursue her dreams of writing sensual happily ever afters.

The desire to fill her world with wonderful stories she and her close friends could not just talk about but gush over keeps Anna's fingers racing to keep up with her imagination. As the rest of the house is sleeping peacefully, Anna sheds her title as Supermom of Three to write sexy love stories

Sleeping might still be a battle Anna hasn't conquered, but armed with a B. A. in English Literature and all the hot men in her mind calling for their own story, she stays busy during those midnight hours writing her next international bestselling spicy romance.

Visit *www.AnnaLoresAuthor.com* for more information and to sign up for Anna's VIP Newsletter.